Red October

RED OCTOBER

The Russian Revolution and the Communist Horizon

Jodi Dean
Amar Farooqui
Irfan Habib
Prakash Karat
Shahrzad Mojab
Prabhat Patnaik
EDITED BY Vijay Prashad
Prabir Purkayastha
B.T. Ranadive
Sitaram Yechury

LeftWord

First published in June 2017
on occasion of EMS Smrithi,
Thrissur, Kerala
Reprinted July 2017

LeftWord Books
2254/2A Shadi Khampur
New Ranjit Nagar
New Delhi 110008
INDIA

LeftWord Books is the publishing division of
Naya Rasta Publishers Pvt. Ltd.

leftword.com

ISBN 978-93-80118-58-1

For publication histories of individual essays,
see Acknowledgements.

Printed and bound by Chaman Enterprises, Delhi

CONTENTS

PART III. The Present

INTRODUCTION

Vijay Prashad

To call for the overthrow of the existing order
May seem a terrible thing
But what exists is no order.
To seek refuge in violence
May seem evil.
But what is constantly at work is violence
And there is nothing special about it.
Communism is not the extreme outlier
That only in a small part can be realized,
and until it is not completely realized,
The situation is unbearable
Even for someone who is insensitive.
Communism is really the most minimal demand
What is nearest, reasonable, the middle term.
Whoever is opposed to it is not someone who thinks otherwise
It is someone who does not think or who thinks only about
    himself
It is an enemy of the human species who,
Terrible
Evil
Insensitive
And, in particular,
Wanting the most extreme, realized even in the tiniest part,
Plunges all humankind into destruction.

Bertolt Brecht, 'Communism is the Middle Term', 1931

The Russian Revolution tore through the fabric of time. What should never have been became real – a workers' state, a country whose dynamic was to be controlled by the working-class and peasantry. It was not enough to overthrow the Tsar and to inaugurate the rule of the bourgeoisie. Too much sacrifice of the people had gone into the uprisings of 1917. That is why a second revolution took place that year. The Soviets seized power. They proclaimed to the world's wretched that this was possible: a country could be ruled by its working people.

Even more remarkable, the new Soviet Union declared that it was not merely to uphold the national interests of the people of the USSR. 'We claim that the interests of socialism, the interests of world socialism, rank higher than national interests, higher than the interests of the state', said Lenin to the Communist Party's Central Committee in May 1918. It was this attitude that moved the Russian communists to create the Communist International (1919-1943). The Russian Revolution was certainly Russian, but its promise was global.

WORKER'S STATE

Human history gives us few examples of toilers taking hold of government. Kings and Queens saw it as their divine right to rule. The French Revolution of 1789 set aside this expectation. Ordinary people – the mob – pushed themselves out of hunger and war to demand the right to rule. Liberty, Equality, Fraternity was their battle cry. Like the Russian Revolution of 1917, the French Revolution's siren was heard far and wide. In the island of Hispaniola, Toussaint L'ouverture – born into slavery – led a rebellion of slaves against the French planters. It was the first successful slave rebellion to form a state. There is a direct line that links these late 18th century rebellions – in France and in Haiti – to the Russian Revolution of 1917. These are its precursors. These rebellions broke the spell of divinity that surrounded the rulers. Ordinary people could rule. That was the lesson of the French and the Haitian Revolutions.

But these revolts of the 18th century took place against

early forms of capitalism – when property was being shaped into capital and when merchants dominated over nascent forms of industry. Through the decades after these revolts, the advantages of colonialism, slavery and trade came to the industrialists. These people used the profits of trade and colonialism to reshape production of goods and services. Harnessing the best of science and technology and taking advantage of workers displaced from farming, the industrialists shaped factory-based production to accumulate more wealth and power. The industrialists and the merchants – the bourgeoisie, in sum – took control not only over the economy, but also of politics. What the ordinary people had done in the French and Haitian Revolution was to overthrow the monarchy, but they were not able to shape history in their image. They delivered their prize to the bourgeoisie.

Competitive capitalism produced rapid developments in technology and in production. Vast amounts of goods were created at the same time as the bourgeoisie put immense pressure on workers to earn less and work more. There emerged quite rapidly a problem of overproduction (too many goods produced) and underconsumption (too few goods purchased) – workers toiled to make the plethora of goods, but earned far too little to buy them back. One crisis after another tore through the system. Karl Marx's *Capital* (1867) assessed the endemic nature of the crises precisely. Marx saw that capitalism was both devilishly productive and dangerously unstable. It impoverished workers to produce a grand civilization, but through this impoverishment it undercut its own ability to survive. Solutions to these crises came through the expansion of national militaries and through wars for colonialism and for markets. Famine for the workers was mirrored in the feasts for the bourgeoisie. It was in this context that the heirs of the French and Haitian Revolutions emerged – the workers' movement in the industrial belts and the anti-colonial peasant and worker movement in the colonies. These twin movements would later form the heart of international communism.

It was the Great War of 1914-1918 that set the clock faster for international communism. At a small gathering in Zimmerwald, Switzerland, in 1915, the socialists offered a unique – Marxist – interpretation of World War I. In their Zimmerwald Manifesto, drafted by Lenin, Alexandra Kollontai and Karl Radek, they wrote, 'Irrespective of the truth as the direct responsibility for the outbreak of the war, one thing is certain: *The war which has produced this chaos is the outcome of imperialism*, of the attempt on the part of the capitalist classes of each nation to foster their greed for profit by exploitation of human labour and of the natural treasures of the entire globe'. This war was not a war of the people, but a war against the people. The Zimmerwald Left urged the working classes to resist the wars, to defy their rulers and create a society in their own image.

The fire hot contradictions of the war provoked a serious crisis in the weakest link of the imperialist chain – in Tsarist Russia. An International Women's Day demonstration on 8 March 1917 set off the workers of the main cities into full-scale rebellion. The International Women's Day march had been a staple of the world socialist movement. In 1917, the Petrograd Interdistrict Committee released a pamphlet, calling on women workers to go on strike. It is an impassioned document, whose flavour can be gleaned from these paragraphs,

> Comrades, working women, for whose sake is a war waged? Do we need to kill millions of Austrian and German workers and peasants? German workers did not want to fight either. Our close ones do not go willingly to the front. They are forced to go. The Austrian, English, and German workers go just as unwillingly. Tears accompany them in their countries as in ours. War is waged for the sake of gold, which glitters in the eyes

> of capitalists, who profit from it. Ministers, mill owners, and bankers hope to fish in troubled waters. They become rich in wartime. After the war, they will not pay military taxes. Workers and peasants will bear all the sacrifices and pay all the costs.
>
> Dear women comrades, will we keep on tolerating this silently for very long, with occasional outbursts of boiling rage against small-time traders? Indeed, it is not they who are at fault for the people's calamities. They have ruined themselves. The government is guilty. It began this war and cannot end it. It ravages the country. It is its fault that you are starving. The capitalists are guilty. It is waged for their profit. It's well-nigh time to shout to them: Enough! Down with the criminal government and its entire gang of thieves and murderers. Long live peace![1]

The Committee did not expect the reaction from the working-women. They left their factories in the thousands. Working-men and slowly the peasantry came alongside them. Soldiers, who came from these classes, joined in. They decided that this war was not their war. Their real war was against the aristocracy and its authoritarian state. That had to be confronted directly. Two days after International Women's Day, fifty thousand workers in St. Petersburg were on strike. It was the most powerful demonstration of worker power in Russia till date. The Tsarist system collapsed on 16 March, just over a week after the International Women's Day demonstrations.

Confidence that workers could govern had to be built. Things moved slowly. The first government to take power was headed by an aristocrat – Prince Georgy Yevgenievich Lvov – and then by a liberal lawyer – Alexander Kerensky.

[1] The pamphlet was translated by Barbara C. Allen and can be found at the LeftWord Books website, http://mayday.leftword.com/blog/100th-anniversary-of-the-1917s-working-womens-day/.

The workers did not go home. The energy of the revolution was quite ferocious. They formed Soviets – Councils – that developed 'dual power', a situation where they created their own institutions that had legitimacy from popular acclamation. Lenin understood that this new situation was the making of the workers. It was their innovation. 'The most highly remarkable feature of our revolution', he wrote in April 1917, 'is that it has brought about a *dual power*. This fact must be grasped foremost: unless it is understood, we cannot advance. We must know how to supplement and amend old formulas, for example, those of Bolshevism, for while they have been found to be correct on the whole, their concrete realisation *has turned out to be* different. *Nobody* previously thought, or could have thought, of a dual power.'

What was 'dual power'? The workers could accept the rule of the Provisional Government, then run by Kerenskey and the bourgeoisie. But parallel to that Government, the workers created their own government – the Soviet of Workers' and Soldiers' Deputies. This was a parliament of the working-class and the peasantry, not a parliament of the merchants, industrialists and their service class. Lenin saw that this new form – the Soviet – had a direct ancestor in the Paris Commune of 1871. What he did not know is that this form of rule had other ancestors – such as the communes (*quilombo*) created by the insurrection of the slaves in Brazil. These are examples from our past of working people creating their own forms of rule – often democratic – against the hierarchies of the masters of property.

What was of great importance is that the workers found their intellectual in Lenin, who listened carefully to what was on-going in the factories and the streets and drove the Bolsheviks towards the mood of the workers. The point, he wrote in April, is not the seizure of power by a minority – for that would be merely an unpopular coup. 'We are Marxists', he wrote, 'we stand for proletarian class struggle against petty bourgeois intoxication, against chauvanism-defencism, phrase-mongering and dependence on the bourgeoisie.' The goal of the Marxists should be to harness the actual experience of the workers and drive an agenda that would make the worker and peasant power into the power of society.

It was precisely this agenda that found its fruition in October, when a second Russian Revolution broke out. This was a seizure of power by the Soviets, who dismissed the bourgeois parliament (the Duma) and appointed themselves as the governors of their own society. Lenin went to the Petrograd Soviet to celebrate the seizure of power. What was the significance of this revolution, he asked his comrade workers? 'Its significance is, first of all, that we shall have a Soviet government, our own organ of power, in which the bourgeoisie will have no share whatsoever. The oppressed masses will themselves create a power. The old state apparatus will be shattered to its foundations and a new administrative apparatus set up in the form of the Soviet organizations.'

From great poverty and deprivation, the USSR quit the Great War, fought off the invasion of the capitalist powers and struggled to build up the industrial and agricultural capacity of the country. Within a decade, the USSR was able to move from extreme backwardness to a situation of economic and social stability. Jawaharlal Nehru visited the country in 1927, exactly ten years after the Russian Revolution. What he saw surprised him, that there was little poverty in the country and that the leadership had come from amongst the workers and peasants. Mikhail Kalinin, whom Nehru met, came from a peasant family and was then the head of state of the USSR. Joseph Stalin, the head of government, came from a family of cobblers and housemaids. These were ordinary people, who now ran an extraordinarily large country. Of his visit, Nehru wrote,

> Russia thus interests us, because it may help us to find some solution for the serious problems which the world faces today. It interests us specially because conditions there have not been, and are not even now, very dissimiliar to conditions in India. Both are vast agricultural countries with only the beginning of industrialization, and both have to face poverty and illiteracy. If Russia finds a satisfactory solution for these, our work in India would be made easier.[2]

In fact, the USSR did find solutions for these problems. In 1897 – in the last Tsarist census – less than a third of Russians counted as literate (only 13% of women were literate). Immense amount of the social surplus in the USSR was turned over to education and health, to the basic needs of the population. By 1937, two decades into the Revolution, the literacy levels rose to 86% for men and 65% for women. It was an extraordinary achievement. It needs to be mentioned that the USSR followed the policy of indigenization (*korenizatsiya*) – promoting regional languages so that people could develop their knowledge and wisdom in their native tongues and not merely in Russian. Nothing like this was done in Nehru's India.

ANTI-COLONIAL MOVEMENT

Russia had long been an inspiration for the anti-colonial world. The 1905 Russian Revolution – which failed – provoked serious reflection from Mahatma Gandhi who was then in South Africa. He watched as the Russian people rose up against the Tsar and marvelled at their courage. 'The

[2] Jawaharlal Nehru, *Soviet Russia: Some Random Sketches and Impressions*, Allahabad: Allahabad Law Journal Press, 1928, p. 5.

Russian workers and all the other servants declared a general strike and stopped all work', Gandhi wrote at that time.[3] The general strike forced the Tsar to make some concessions, for – as Gandhi noted – 'it is not within the power of even the Tsar of Russia to force strikers to return at the point of bayonet. For even the powerful cannot rule without the cooperation of the ruled.' Gandhi watched both the Russian Revolution and the *Swadeshi* agitation in Bengal. Both seemed linked to him. 'The movement in Bengal for the use of *swadeshi* goods is much like the Russian movement', he wrote. 'Our shackles will break this very day, if the people of India become united and patient, love their country, and think of the well-being of their motherland disregarding their self-interest. The governance of India is possible only because there exist people who serve. We also can show that same strength that the Russian people have done.'

The Russian Revolution of 1917 sent out an even sharper message. It won. That was significant. But it also produced a genuine workers and peasants' government. Faced with a sharp attack from the imperialist powers, the Communists in Russia realised that their revolution could only survive if it was met with other revolutions. They initially thought that a revolution would break out in Germany. When the hope of this faded, they turned to the colonial world. The Comintern, set up in 1919, had as its mission the spread of communism across the planet. The Comintern gave material assistance to revolutionary fighters from the Americas to Africa to Asia. It was this vast international network that provided a boost for the anti-colonial struggles, which had been on-going for a generation. It might be worth saying that the decolonization wave happened – to some extent – because of the siren of

[3] For this, and subsequent quotes from Gandhi, see his 'Russia and India', *Indian Opinion*, 28 October 1905, 11 November 1905 and 8 September 1906.

the USSR and because of the material support provided by the Comintern to various movements from China to the Gold Coast.

A HUNDRED YEARS LATER

The USSR was never given a chance. From its first days, it was criticized mercilessly. Sitting in his Turkish exile in 1930, Leon Trotsky wrote his magisterial *History of the Russian Revolution*. Thirteen years had elapsed since the October Revolution. The revolution was already being derided. 'Capitalism', Trotsky wrote in his conclusion, 'required a hundred years to elevate science and technique to the heights and plunge humanity into the hell of war and crisis. To socialism its enemies allow only fifteen years to create and furnish a terrestrial paradise. We took no such obligation upon ourselves. We never set these dates. The process of vast transformation must be measured by an adequate scale.' But it did not have the time to develop.

The USSR lasted only seventy years. This is a very small period of time in the scope of world history. Its achievements have been pilloried – its demise being the greatest argument against its achievements. But merely because it disappeared does not mean that it was without merit. It provides us with the assurance that a workers and peasants' state can exist, that it can create policies to benefit the vast masses of the people rather than merely the rich, that it can heal and educate rather than merely starve and kill. This is something to hold on to.

Of course there were several problems with the USSR, some of which led to its demise. That the Bolsheviks created a monopoly of power and did not allow other parties to exist suffocated political life. It meant that there was simply not sufficient space for criticism of policy. Such criticism is enriching – it enables humans to know if they are on the right track, to test their own certainties. That the USSR had to create a massive military apparatus to protect themselves from armed attack meant that scarce resources had to be diverted from social development. A capitalist system is geared toward military production and war, whereas a socialist system should abjure this dynamic. But faced with threats, the USSR had to go in a direction that greatly distorted its possibilities.

The Soviet Union collapsed in 1991. The great social wealth was then turned over to an oligarchy. The social deterioration was rapid. The British medical journal – *The Lancet* – estimated that over a million Russians died 'due to the economic shock of mass privatization and shock therapy' in the decade from 1991 to 2001.[4] Life expectancy for the Russian male was 65 in the last days of the USSR, but it collapsed to 60 a decade later. Inequality and sorrow returned to the new republics that emerged out of the USSR. No wonder then that polls routinely find that more than half of the Russian citizens dream of a return to the days of the USSR.

READING THE USSR

This book is not, of course, a comprehensive account of the Russian Revolution or of its aftermath. However, it is a source-book of some important essays which lead us through its experience. Part 1 opens with the Revolution itself – with historians Irfan Habib and Amar Farooqui giving us their interpretations of the Revolution (Habib) and its impact on the colonial world (Farooqui). These are lyrical essays, offering a window into a complex set of events and into debates over these events. The impact of the Revolution was monumental. India was rattled by the Revolution, not only because it

[4] David Stuckler, Lawrence King and Martin McKee, 'Mass Privatization and the Post-Communist Mortality Crisis: a Cross-National Analysis', *The Lancet*, Vol. 373, no. 9661, 2009.

inaugurated a workers' state, but also because it took an unequivocal position against imperialism. In December 1917, when he got word of the enormity of the Revolution, the journalist K. P. Khadilkar wrote,

> In November, power in Petrograd passed into the hands of those socialists who were led by Lenin and who want a separate peace treaty with Germany. Kerensky and his cabinet have been dethroned from power. The call for the uprising was given by Lenin's supporters among the sailors in the gulf of Finland. Kerensky has fled. Lenin has secured power in Petrograd, Moscow, and the surrounding regions. The soldiers are also supporting him. Lenin has issued a decree declaring the rights of nations to self-determination, and freedom has been given to the Baltic states and the Polish people to exercise the right (*Chitramaya-jagat*, December 1917).

Khadilkar watched events in Russia with great interest, seeing the emergence of the USSR as a great beacon for the anti-colonial struggles. When US President Woodrow Wilson tried to take credit for the idea of peace without annexations and for self-determination, Khadilkar wrote, 'Lenin did it more than two years ago'.[5]

Gandhi, who was very critical of Communism, nonetheless acknowledged a decade after the Revolution, 'There is no questioning the fact that the Bolshevik ideal has behind it the purest sacrifice of countless men and women, who have given up their all for its sake; an ideal that is sanctified by sacrifices of such master spirits as Lenin cannot go in vain' (*Young India*, 5 November 1928).

Part II of this book goes back to the diagnosis of important

[5] For this, and the previous quote, see S. G. Sardesai, *India and the Russian Revolution*, New Delhi: CPI, 1967, pp. 18-21.

Indian Marxists and Communists of the USSR's collapse. I recall reading these essays from *The Marxist*, and being oriented by them to the bewildering events in the East. What did *perestroika* (restructuring) and *glasnost* (openness) mean? What were these currents of 'reform' inside the Soviet Union, which seemed to spiral out of control? On 31 December 1991, the USSR was dissolved. Nikolai Ryzhkov, the last Chair of the Council of Minister, said of the dissolution that it was 'the greatest tragedy of the 20th century'. The seventy-year experiment with socialism came to an end. When the Paris Commune fell to the guns of tyranny in May 1871, Marx wrote *The Civil War in France* (June 1871) to take the temperature of the collapse. No such full assessment has been produced from a Marxist standpoint of the fall of the USSR – even decades after the fact. These essays – by B. T. Ranadive, Prakash Karat and Sitaram Yechury, in Part II, written as events unfolded in the USSR, remain some of the best pathfinders to explain the crisis in the USSR and the reasons for its collapse.

Part III of the book brings us to the present – to the future of the Revolutionary project, with essays of great insight and range from Prabhat Patnaik on the current form of globalization, from Jodi Dean on the imperative of the Party, from Prabir Purkayastha on how to create a socialist imagination in these post-Fordist times and from Shahrzad Mojab on the requirement that a revolutionary project be as expansive as possible in terms of its horizon.

Red October is an invitation to rediscover the importance of the Russian Revolution, to explore how it faltered and to nudge us to consider the ghosts of that revolution in our own movements today.

PART I

THE REVOLUTION

Proletarians
arrive at communism
from below –
by the low way of mines,
sickles,
and pitchforks –
But I,
from poetry's skies,
plunge into communism,
because
without it
I feel no love.

Vladimir Mayakovsky, 'Back Home', 1925

THE ROAD TO THE OCTOBER REVOLUTION IN RUSSIA, 1917

Irfan Habib

After the British Empire, it was the Russian Empire before 1917 which by territorial extent formed the largest state in the world. Within it, Russia was both in extent and population the dominant country. Going by its European part alone, it also formed the largest country of Europe, containing in 1913 some 120 million Russian speaking people, dwarfing the population of every other European country. Yet Russia was in terms of every economic index among the most backward and poorest of European countries. Its per capita income in 1913 was about 102 roubles, compared to that of England, 463 roubles, France, 355, and Germany, 292. It depended mainly on agriculture, which contributed 51.3 per cent of the total national income, while industry contributed only 28.0 per cent. Modern industry had developed, but in so large a country pig iron production in 1913 amounted only to 4.6 million tons, compared to Germany's 16.8 million tons. Converted into rates per capita, Russia smelted only 30 kg of pig iron, compared to Germany, 250 kg, and England, 206 kg. The industrial working class, counting only people dependent on factory-manufacturing and mining, comprised only 2 per cent of the population, i.e., only 3.3 million spread all over the Russian Empire. Eighty per cent of the population was dependent on agriculture, and less than a fifth of the population lived in towns.

Industry in Russia was, as elsewhere, largely under the control of private capitalists. There was a strong degree of concentration and various 'syndicates' controlled different sectors of industry and commerce. There was also much foreign capital: in 1914 direct foreign investments in industry and mining amounted to 2.3 billion roubles, and total net foreign debt to 7.5 billion roubles or US $ 3.8 billion. In agriculture landlords occupied large areas of land with extensive tenantry. The so-called communes (*mir*) where land was periodically redistributed began to be abandoned as a result of 'Stolypin Reforms', 1906-12, which greatly encouraged farming by rich peasants (kulaks) and increased the number of landless labourers.

Over and above this lop-sided backwardness was the system of autocracy headed by the Tsar who governed through a landed nobility and bureaucracy and a large army. The parliamentary trappings of European countries were absent until 1906, whereafter too the Duma (Russian parliament) had little real power.

With all its backwardness, Russia had one redeeming feature. It had a fairly extensive educational system: In 1913, as many as 68 per cent of its military recruits (mainly from amongst peasants) were found to be literate. It had a large intelligentsia including scientists and engineers and a large body of technically competent intellectuals, who closely followed the ideological and cultural trends of Western Europe.

It was the existence of such an intelligentsia that explains an early presence of socialist ideas. The Populists ('Narodniks') were followers of Herzen (1812-70), who came to believe that the Russian village commune could be converted into a nucleus of socialist society so that Russia might be able to avoid the exploitative system of capitalism once it had liberated itself from Tsarist autocracy. Marx's critique of capitalism naturally attracted the attention of Herzen's followers. Danielson, a Narodnik, translated Marx's *Capital*, Vol. I, into Russian, publishing it in 1872, within four years of the original German edition. Karl Marx (d. 1883) himself in his late years thought that given its peasant unrest, Russia was the country where a revolution was then impending, so that it is wrong to hold that the October Revolution of 1917 occurred in contradiction to Marx's own predictions. However, despite the Narodniks' efforts to go among the people – a deliberate campaign to physically do so was launched by them in the 1870s – their unrealistic commune-oriented romanticism and resort to individual terror ultimately undermined their movement, and they ceased to be important well before 1900. (Their ideological positions were heavily attacked by Lenin in *What the 'Friends of the People' Are*, 1893, and *Development of Capitalism in Russia*, 1899.)

The space vacated by Narodniks was then occupied from about 1890s, by three trends, all owing allegiance to Marxism. The 'Legal Marxists', led by P. B. Struve, claimed that by simply bringing Marx's doctrine to the notice of the Russian public, without indulging in any revolutionary activity themselves, they were still serving to spread its message. The second trend, dubbed 'Economism' by Lenin, was that of people who thought that the revolution could be only brought about by the working class and, therefore, the main field of action lay in organizing trade unions and fighting for the workers' day-to-day demands. This, in Lenin's view, meant ultimately that the working-class movement would just remain confined to winning some concessions from capitalism. But the Russian Revolution of 1905 was in fact ignited by the practically spontaneous actions of workers, who rose against the Tsar's government and created the 'soviets', or workers' councils as organs of workers' power, however short-lived these might have been at that time.

The third trend was a fully Marxist one of which the founder was G. V. Plekhanov (1856-1918), an important Marxist thinker, who helped to organize, first, the Emancipation of Labour Group and, then, in 1903 at its 'second' congress (after an abortive one in 1895) the Russian Social Democratic Labour Party. Much ground for it was prepared by V. I. Lenin's tract *What is to be Done?*, 1902, in which he had criticized the positions of the Legal Marxists and Economists, and urged the need for a political party of professional revolutionaries, who would infuse the workers with a socialist consciousness, while maintaining discipline and secrecy so necessary under an authoritarian regime.

The Social Democrats who thus came together in 1903 believed that Russia would need to have two successive revolutions. In the first, categorized as 'bourgeois-democratic', something akin to the French Revolution of 1789, Tsardom would be overthrown and replaced by an elected Parliament; and landlords' estates would be divided up among peasants, as had happened in France. There would also be some relief gained for the workers (e.g., limited working day, right to organize, etc.). In the main, capitalism would be strengthened since it would be provided with a mass consumer market in the countryside, and by full protection of capitalist property everywhere. A socialist revolution must therefore follow the bourgeois democratic revolution in order to overthrow the regime of the capitalist class.

Given this broad perspective, right from 1903, two trends developed within the Social Democratic Labour Party, though it took some time for the differences to crystallize. With regard to the two successive revolutions, Lenin and his supporters argued that the revolutionary Social Democrats should themselves work to bring about a bourgeois-democratic revolution, and for this purpose not only rely on workers, but also rally the poorer peasants, among whom landlords' lands would be distributed. This would place the Social Democrats in a position to create a favourable situation for a subsequent socialist revolution, in which the working class (the 'proletariat') would have the poorer strata of peasants and landless labourers as its allies. For such revolutionary activity, it would be necessary to build a disciplined workers' party based on 'democratic centralism'. Broadly this position was supported by the majority of delegates at the second Party Congress in London in 1903 whence the name 'Bolshevik' (majority) becoming the common designation of those who accepted this perspective. The Social Democrats who did not subscribe to it came to be called 'Mensheviks' (minority).

The Mensheviks' views varied. Most of them believed that the bourgeois-democratic revolution would occur because the growth of capitalism was making it inevitable. The task of Social Democrats should be to prepare essentially for the next socialist revolution. Thus unlike Lenin they saw little necessity of making concessions to the peasantry, with its petit-bourgeois ambitions. Nor did they see the need for a well-knit centralized party on which Lenin insisted. In actual fact the issue of the nature of the Party came first, provoking Lenin to issue a pamphlet *One Step Forward, Two Steps Back* (1904).

The 1905 Revolution was remarkable for the fact that a series of spontaneous actions like the mutiny of battleship Potemkin and workers' strikes in the capital St. Petersburg and other cities led to the creation of the 'soviets of workers'. The first of these was the St. Petersburg Soviet of Workers' Deputies, which came to have the fiery Trotsky as its leader. Lenin too returned from exile. But the army still remained with the Tsar, and in December the revolt was forcibly suppressed, while a new 'constitution' was announced creating the Duma or Russian Parliament. Its elections were so structured that one elector would be chosen by 2000 landowners, whereas 30,000 peasants chose one, the number being 90,000 in case of workers. A Duma so elected could only be a rubber-stamp one, but Lenin was to declare later that it had been a mistake to have boycotted the 1906 elections (first) to the Duma.

An obvious reason for the defeat of the 1905 Revolution

was the relative passivity of the peasantry; there was also the fact that neither the Bolsheviks nor Mensheviks yet had extensive organizations among workers. Given the authoritarian nature of the Tsarist regime, Lenin wished the Party to take advantage of every means to spread its message. The Bolsheviks took part in the 1906 (second elections) and subsequent elections (1907 and 1912) to the Duma, despite their securing very few seats owing to the skewed electoral system. But still they had a rostrum, which the Government could not shut them out from, despite the regime of censorship, exile and imprisonment that prevailed in the Stolypin period (1906-12).

In this period the Bolsheviks worked out their strategic position. Lenin wrote a defence of Marxist philosophy in his *Materialism and Empirio-criticism*, 1909. In 1913 he made clear his position on the question of national independence for all countries, including those in the Russian empire, in his *Critical Notes on the National Question*, which J. V. Stalin supplemented by his *Marxism and the National Question* the same year. Up till now in the Second International, to which the Bolsheviks too owed allegiance, the principle of national self-determination had not been conceded, in the name of international solidarity; and even Rosa Luxemburg, the future Communist martyr, criticized Lenin's position. But Lenin believed that true internationalism demanded precisely such a policy; and he was surely mindful also of the grievances of the nationalities in the Russian empire, from Central Asia to Poland. Stalin added another dimension to it, when he saw it as a necessary part of a policy of worker-peasant alliance, arguing that the national question was in effect a 'peasant question'.

While such ideological clarification was going on, the Bolsheviks decided to abandon the nominal adherence to a single party jointly with the Mensheviks. They took this decision at a conference in Prague (then in Austria-Hungary) in January 1912, hereafter calling their Party 'Social-Democratic Labour Party (Bolsheviks)'.

This decision came none too soon, for in July 1914 the First World War broke out, in which Russia joined France and England in a war against Germany, Austria-Hungary and Turkey. The danger of such a war breaking out had loomed for some time, and so as early as 1907 the Second International had resolved that in the event it did break out, the working-class parties must 'utilise the economic and political crises caused by the war to . . . hasten the destruction of the class domination of the capitalist class'. This position was repeated still more firmly in its Basle Manifesto of 1912. But when the war broke out in 1914, all workers' parties in the belligerent countries hastened to support their own national governments, most surprisingly of all, the German Social Democratic Party, whose leaders, with Kautsky at their head, had been so far regarded as the high priests of Marxism. Mensheviks too, with the venerable Plekhanov at the head, rushed to support the Tsar's government in the war it had recklessly embarked upon.

Only Lenin and the Bolsheviks stood firm and never wavered. The Bolshevik deputies in the Duma refused to vote for war credits, and were for their recalcitrance put in prison. Lenin denounced the war, but did not, like the dissident Mensheviks, call simply for peace; he called for civil war, for the defeat of the government of one's own country. In the prevalent spate of jingoism such a position could hardly be popular, and even some Bolshevik leaders like Kamenev demurred. Lenin not only stuck to his position, but wrote perhaps his most influential work, *Imperialism, the Highest Stage of Capitalism* (1916) in which he showed how the war was the result of the drive for monopoly over the world market and for destruction of rival capitalist competitors.[1]

Two and a half years of war on an unprecedented scale brought havoc upon the country and its population. A few statistics can best tell the story. Russia's national income fell from 15.8 billion gold roubles in 1914-15 to 12.2 billion in 1916-17, a fall of nearly 23 per cent, but civilian consumption dropped from 11.5 billion gold roubles to 7.3 billion, a fall of nearly 37 per cent! As between 1 July 1914 and 1 January 1917 currency circulation increased 5.6 times, and the price index rose 7.0 times. Since wages in all industries in current roubles rose from an average of 218 to 406, a rise of less than 1.9 times, one can see that a huge fall in real wages must have occurred over the period.

The Tsarist army, 12 million strong in 1917, was mainly an army recruited from peasants. Some early successes in the war were followed by repeated defeats at the hands of German and Austro-Hungarian troops. By the end of 1916 Poland, Lithuania, much of western White Russia and western Ukraine had been lost, with huge casualties among the soldiers.

The impoverishment of civilians and hardships among soldiers engendered a huge loss of popular confidence in the Tsarist administration, a feeling which extended to the capitalists, many of whom had benefited so much from war contracts, and even to the landed aristocracy. The loss of the Tsar's moral authority was intensified by the affair of an illiterate swindler Rasputin (assassinated, December 1916), and the constant changes of ministries at the Tsar's whims.

While popular unrest grew, as indicated by workers' strikes, the mass influence of Bolsheviks was still limited even among workers. They had, by their hostility to the war, become

[1] V. I. Lenin, *Imperialism: the Highest Stage of Capitalism*, Introduction by Prabhat Patnaik, New Delhi: LeftWord Books, 2000.

the target of government oppression, their leaders thrown into prison or exile in Siberia, and their newspapers like *Pravda* (established, 1912) closed and publications seized. It was with great difficulty that leaders like Stalin who remained in Russia, eluding the police as much as they could, were able to preserve the Party structure intact. The most popular 'Left' party was that of the Socialist Revolutionaries (SR), who had their base mainly among the peasants, while the Mensheviks too, being 'Defencists' or supporters of the War, had obtained considerable official tolerance for their activities.

Popular unrest broke out in the capital, Petrograd (changed name of St. Petersburg, later Leningrad), and the Petrograd Soviet of workers' and soldiers' deputies was formed on 27 February 1917. On the same day a Provisional Committee of the Dissolved Fourth Duma claimed to take over power and on 1 March 1917 a Provisional Government was formed, consisting of landlords, and capitalists, representing the major bourgeois parties, viz. Octoberists and Cadets, supported by Socialist Revolutionaries and Mensheviks, who had a single representative in the ministry, Kerensky. The Ministry was headed characteristically by Prince Lvov, a landlord. Politically, this meant the end of Tsardom. Tsar Nicholas II abdicated, in favour of his brother Michael, who also abdicated. Ultimately, a republic was proclaimed.

Initially, the February Revolution seemed to carry out some elements of a bourgeois-democratic platform. Civil liberty was established, political prisoners were released, and censorship was abolished. The Bolsheviks like others could carry out their activities. Even the working class seemed to have obtained a share in power, as Soviets of workers and soldiers (and, later, of peasants as well) arose everywhere, and a 'Dual Power' was established: the writ of the Provisional Government was modified by that of the local Soviets in most areas. It was clear that what Lenin and others had been stressing was at play now; viz. the political weakness of the Russian bourgeoisie owing to the limited nature of the development of capitalism, a weakness shown previously in relation to the land-owners and now in confronting the working class.

What, however, reinforced the position of the Provisional Government was the cooperation it obtained from both the Socialist Revolutionaries and the Mensheviks who initially controlled the Soviets, the Bolsheviks constituting only a small minority in them. Both these parties supported the war against Germany, and this meant that the major cause of economic distress and soldiers' grievances would continue. As a result of reckless war expenditure, prices rose by 67 per cent between 1 January and 1 October 1917, and real wages declined to 57.4 per cent of the 1916 level.

As the Bolshevik centre was re-established after the February revolutions, Bolshevik leaders within Russia tended to think that with the overthrow of Tsarism, a defensive war could be supported and the provisional Government did not need to be directly opposed. These views were, however, rejected by Lenin when he returned to Russia from exile in April 1917. On 17 April at Petrograd he presented his 'April Theses', in which he first of all rejected the theory of 'revolutionary defencism' to justify support of the war carried on by the Provisional Government.[2] He pointed out that the war still remained an 'imperialist war'. Secondly, he said, 'no support must be given to the Provisional Government'. It had only been the ideological and organizational weakness of the proletariat that had allowed the bourgeoisie to take power. Given this reading, it followed that the working class should organize and press on to convert the bourgeois-democratic revolution into a socialist revolution.

[2] *Revolution! Lenin's 1917 Writings*, edited and introduced by Prakash Karat, New Delhi: LeftWord, forthcoming.

The 'April Theses' henceforth became the main basis of Bolshevik policy, and in July-August 1917 at the sixth Party Congress an economic programme was worked out, which in the main combined bourgeois-democratic features with major socialist elements. Thus landlords' land was to be confiscated and disposed of among poor peasants and labourers, but, by implication, kulaks' lands would not be touched. On the other hand, banks were to be nationalized and 'control' established over insurance companies and the large capitalist syndicates. Only by a gradual transformation thereafter was full workers' 'regulation of production' to be established.

Almost during the same period, August-September, Lenin sat down to compose his *State and Revolution* (actually published next year, 1918). For our present purpose it is important because it underlined the necessity of the 'dictatorship of the proletariat' to be established after a socialist revolution. It is the working class, created by capitalism, on which the responsibility of building socialism would fall, and so after the revolution it must totally reorganize the state for its own purposes. The proletarian state would 'wither away' only when socialism got transformed into communism in the future.

It was thus clear to Lenin that the responsibility for carrying out the socialist revolution and pursuing revolutionary objectives after its success lay on the shoulders of the working-class and its party, which, in the case of Russia, was that of the Bolsheviks. In June 1917 at the first Russian Congress of Soviets, when the Bolsheviks were still behind Mensheviks in strength with 105 seats against their 248, Lenin had boldly retorted, 'There is such a Party – the Bolshevik Party', in response to the Menshevik Tsereteli's claim that there was no party in Russia willing to take the place of the Provisional Government. Incidentally, at this Congress Trotsky with his group solidly supported the Bolsheviks and subsequently, despite his previous invectives against Lenin, he was admitted to the top leadership of the Bolshevik Party, to play a leading part in the October Revolution.

In July the Provisional Government ordered the arrest of Lenin and other Bolshevik leaders. Lenin went underground. The Sixth Party Congress of the Bolsheviks was held in July-August, largely guided by Stalin, who made it clear that a socialist revolution in the near future was on the Party's agenda.

An episode hastened the pace of events. On 25 August the recently dismissed Commander-in-Chief Kornilov attempted a coup against the Provisional Government, now headed by Kerensky. The Bolsheviks, fearing a royalist restoration, mobilized workers in Petrograd, formed armed Red Guard detachments and had railway workers help stop or divert military trains carrying Kornilov's troops. Kornilov's coup collapsed as many of his troops themselves abandoned his cause.

Success in the Kornilov affair showed how strong the Bolsheviks had become. In April 1917 the Party membership was barely 80,000; by middle of August it had risen to 250,000; and at the beginning of October it reached 400,000 – growing five times within six months. By now the Bolsheviks had obtained majorities in the Petrograd and Moscow Soviets, and they were also expected to command majority support at the Second Congress of Soviets due to meet on 25 October (old calendar) corresponding to 7 November by the new or international calendar adopted after the October Revolution. Red Guards, armed workers and soldiers under the banner of the Petrograd Soviet overthrew the Provisional Government and installed the Bolshevik Government under the slogan 'all Power to the Soviets'. The story of the stirring events that now took place and the superb leadership displayed by Lenin and his colleagues is brought out by an American eyewitness, John Reed in his *Ten Days That Shook the World*.[3]

While the heroism and determination with which the revolution was carried out, which Reed so well brings out, will remain an ever-alive epic, we must also take a view of what the balance of forces was in the political sphere in the country at large. One index of this is offered by the elections to the Constituent Assembly held under the old bureaucracy all over the country within a week of the Revolution.

These elections showed that the Bolsheviks had practically ousted the Mensheviks from the ranks of the working class. They obtained 175 seats to the Mensheviks' 16. But among the peasants they had yet to obtain a foothold. The Socialist Revolutionaries got only 4,696 votes (against 424,027 for the Bolsheviks) in the capital Petrograd, but were massively favoured by the peasants, obtaining 410 seats in the Constituent Assembly. An effort by Bolsheviks to take into alliance the Left Socialist Revolutionaries as representatives of the poor peasantry was only partly and temporarily successful. It was clear that if the Bolsheviks wished to secure peasant support in order to defend the Revolution itself, the socialist revolution would in part have also to complete, the bourgeois – democratic revolution and give peasants their rights. Thus on the very second day of the Revolution came the decree on land. All lands and livestock, farm buildings and implements owned by the landlords were held forfeit without compensation to be managed or distributed by Land Committees or Peasant Soviets. All rents paid by peasants to landlords were abolished. Peasants thus gained 150 million hectares of land, and were relieved of a rent burden of 500 million gold roubles a year. The other decree (in fact the

[3] John Reed, *Ten Days that Shook the World*, preface by P. Sainath, New Delhi: LeftWord Books, forthcoming.

first) was on peace, demanding a cessation of war without annexations and allowing national self-determination. Such peace was exactly what the peasants in uniform also wanted.

For workers came a decree of 12 November imposing an eight-hour working day. The first real step towards creating a socialist sector in the economy was taken on 10 November a decree on worker's control over factories. Other measures extending state control were followed by a decree on 14 December nationalizing all banks.

Another important decree was issued on 2 November 1917 by which Russian colonial rule stood abolished and all nations within Russia were given the right of self-determination. Soviet Russia thus became a beacon-light for national liberation movements throughout the world.

The power of the Soviets quickly spread all over the country. This was real democracy at work, as workers and peasants freely took decisions subject to the centre's decrees. But after a very unfavourable treaty with Germany (Brest-Litovsk, March 1918) came the Allied Intervention and the Civil War that the Allies instigated. The Red Army was created to defend the Soviet fatherland and, at enormous human cost, it defeated thirteen foreign armies and the troops of the revolting 'white' generals. By 1920 all enemies had been suppressed or driven out. Soviet Russia at last could now restore its economy under Lenin's New Economic Policy. Lenin himself died in January 1924, but the Soviet people continued on the path he had set them on. In 1928 began the epic construction of a state-owned industrialized economy and collective farming, without any element of exploitation or private profit. Socialism was thus fully established in the Soviet Union when the First Five-year Plan ended in 1933. This was a unique achievement in world history and marked the fulfilment of the main object of the great October Revolution.

THE OCTOBER REVOLUTION AND THE NATIONAL MOVEMENT IN INDIA

Amar Farooqui

The Great October Socialist Revolution was of momentous significance for the oppressed peoples of the world. It inspired new revolutionary movements; radicalized people's struggles; and had a profound impact on national liberation movements. Further, it made Marxism – Leninism a potent ideological force internationally. By the end of the First World War the old imperialist powers, particularly Britain and France, were exhausted and much weakened. They could no longer rule over their colonies with the same coercive methods that they had employed for over nearly two centuries. The Russian Revolution demonstrated the need for mobilizing masses, for organizing peasants and workers, to intensify the struggle against colonial exploitation. It is not surprising that there were mass upheavals extending from Egypt to China in the years immediately following the success of the October Revolution. The 1919 uprising in Egypt led by Zaglul Pasha forced the British to accept the sovereign status of the country; the March First Movement in Korea in 1919 against Japanese rule was a decisive moment in the struggle for Korean independence; the widespread revolt of 1920 against British rule in Iraq could only be suppressed through extensive aerial bombardment; and the Mongolian Revolution of 1921 made Mongolia the second socialist state in the world (1924).

In China, the May Fourth Movement which began in 1919, and which had its roots in the intellectual and cultural resurgence in the years following the 1911 revolution that had led to the establishment of the republic, was a crucial stage in the fight against imperialism. The movement rapidly acquired a popular character, paving the way for the emergence of the Chinese Communist Party in 1921. The influence of the Russian Revolution was vital in shaping these developments in China. In Turkey, between 1919 and 1922, nationalist forces under the leadership of Kemal Ataturk were engaged in a prolonged campaign against the military onslaught of imperialist powers which had been victorious in the war. Turkey became a republic in 1923, following which a wide-ranging reform programme was initiated by the new republican state over which Kemal Ataturk presided for the next fifteen years. The active assistance of the Bolshevik government was a major factor in the success of nationalists in defending the independence of Turkey; continuing Russian support guaranteed stability, enabling radical reforms to be undertaken under the leadership of Kemal Ataturk. The historical role of socialist Russia in the emergence of modern Turkey was conveniently forgotten by subsequent right-wing regimes. The national liberation struggle in French Indo-China, especially Vietnam, acquired a revolutionary thrust under the influence of the October Revolution. The establishment of the socialist state in Russia, and Lenin's understanding of the colonial question, propelled Ho Chi Minh in the direction of Marxism and Bolshevism. Ho Chi Minh was in France when World War I came to an end. Woodrow Wilson's empty rhetoric about the right of peoples to self-determination had no concrete implications for the independence of French Indo-China. Around 1919, Ho Chi Minh began organizing for the struggle against colonial rule in Vietnam, laying the foundations of a prolonged resistance led by Communists which was to eventually decisively trounce three imperialist powers – Japan, France and USA. In later years, recalling his ideological initiation Ho Chi Minh stated,

> After World War I, I made my living in Paris . . . . I would distribute leaflets denouncing the crimes committed by the French colonialists in Viet Nam. At that time, I supported the

> October Revolution only instinctively, not yet grasping all its historic importance. I loved and admired Lenin because he was a great patriot who liberated his compatriots; until then, I had read none of his books. . . . [Then] a comrade gave me Lenin's 'Theses on the national and colonial questions' published by *l'Humanite* to read. There were political terms difficult to understand in this thesis. But by dint of reading it again and again, finally I could grasp the main part of it. What emotion, enthusiasm, clear-sightedness and confidence it instilled into me! I was overjoyed to tears. Though sitting alone in my room, I shouted out aloud as if addressing large crowds: 'Dear martyrs compatriots! This is what we need, this is the path to our liberation!'[1]

During the war, Social Democratic parties, including the once great German Social Democratic Party, supported their respective governments in what was essentially a conflict between imperialist powers for a redivision of the world, thereby betraying the cause of socialism. In this historical situation it was envisaged that national liberation movements in colonies would have a much bigger, and more important, role to play in the worldwide struggle against imperialism and capitalism. This was underlined by Lenin in *Imperialism: The Highest Stage of Capitalism*. The struggle against colonial rule was very much part of revolutionary movements seeking to overthrow capitalism, and was closely linked with proletarian struggles in advanced capitalist countries. Perhaps for the time being the latter had been much weakened, something that had to be recognized after the defeat of the German Revolution, and the brutal assassination of its leaders Rosa Luxemburg and Karl Liebknecht in early 1919. In his *Draft Theses on*

[1] Ho Chi Minh, 'The Path Which Led Me to Leninism', 1960, *Selected Works of Ho Chi Minh*, Vol.IV.

the National and Colonial Questions (June 1920) Lenin clearly spelt out the position of the Communist International (Comintern), at its Second Congress, on this issue:

> The world political situation has now placed the dictatorship of the proletariat on the order of the day. World political developments are of necessity concentrated on a single focus – the struggle of the world bourgeoisie against the Soviet Russian Republic, around which are inevitably grouped, on the one hand, the Soviet movements of the advanced workers in all countries, and, on the other, all the national liberation movements in the colonies and among the oppressed nationalities, who are learning from bitter experience that their only salvation lies in the Soviet system's victory over world imperialism. Consequently, one cannot at present confine oneself to a bare recognition or proclamation of the need for closer union between the working people of the various nations: a policy must be pursued that will achieve the closest alliance, with Soviet Russia, of all the national and colonial liberation movements. The form of this alliance should be determined by the degree of development of the communist movement in the proletariat of each country, or of the bourgeois-democratic liberation movement of the workers and peasants in backward countries or among backward nationalities.

In India, news of the October Revolution was received with great interest and excitement among nationalists. By 1917 there was growing resentment over the massive use of India's resources in a war that was being fought for furthering Britain's imperial interests. Apart from money and supplies, India was forced to contribute nearly 15 lakh soldiers as part of its war effort. The soldiers fought in distant theatres, in the killing fields of Europe, Ypres (in present-day Belgium) for instance, under the most appalling conditions, for a cause that ultimately would prolong the subjugation of the Indian people. About 75,000 Indian soldiers were killed in the fighting. The colonial authorities resorted to coercive measures to procure supplies of Indian soldiers as cannon fodder. Informally conscription was introduced in major recruiting zones such as Punjab, where quotas for enlistment were imposed on villages. This led to widespread disaffection that would become a significant factor in the popular anti-colonial post-war upsurge in Punjab.

It was against this backdrop that the British government announced that some concession would be made to nationalist sentiment after the war. In August 1917 Edwin Montagu, as secretary of state for India, officially declared in the House of Commons that Britain was committed to 'the gradual development of self-governing institutions with a view to the progressive realization of responsible government in India'. This was followed by the Montagu – Chelmsford Report of 1918, which in turn led to the Government of India Act of 1919. The key feature of the report and the act was a constitutional scheme of limited autonomy for provincial governments. These governments were supposedly answerable to provincial legislative assemblies, elected on the basis of a severely restricted franchise. In practice the provincial governments remained firmly under British control. A few subjects, such as education and health, were 'transferred' to these governments. In any case the colonial state hardly had any interest in these areas of governance.

The timing of the Montagu declaration and the Montagu – Chelmsford Report is noteworthy. The declaration came within a few months of the February Revolution in Russia. The so-called 'reforms', which the report offered, were seen as a necessary sop to prevent the radicalization of the national movement due to Bolshevik influence. The report itself acknowledged that the revolution in Russia 'was regarded in

India as a triumph over despotism' and had 'given an impetus to Indian political aspirations'. Several sections of nationalists in India were aware of the immense historical significance of what was happening in Russia. Shortly after the February revolution the Allahabad-based *Abhyudaya*, of which Madan Mohan Malaviya was the guiding spirit, wrote in an issue of March 1917 that 'The Russian revolution convinces us that there is no power in the world which an animating and life-giving nationalism could not have overcome'.

However it was the October Revolution that really enthused the nationalists. As might have been expected there was a vicious propaganda offensive by the colonial state against the Bolsheviks. This itself motivated nationalists to identify with the Bolshevik cause. Lenin came to be regarded as the leader not just of the Russian people but of oppressed people throughout the world. Tilak came out strongly in defence of Lenin in *Kesari* (29 January 1918), denouncing British slander against him and praising the Russian Revolution. Subramania Bharati composed an ode, 'New Russia', celebrating the revolution:

> Life of the people as they themselves order it.
> A law to uplift the life of the common man.
> Now are there no bonds of slavery.
> No slaves exist now.

In 1920-21, R. S. Avasthi published several popular booklets in Hindi on the subject. These included *Russian Revolution* and *Lenin: His Life and His Thoughts*. G. V. Krishna Rao's *Nikolai Lenin: His Life and Activities* came out from Madras in 1921. Another biographical account penned by B. I. Bhargava, entitled *Lenin*, was published from Lucknow in 1922. Together these, and several other writings spread the message of the October Revolution. There was growing admiration for the Russian communists, and their statements and actions were followed carefully.

On 8 November 1917 the Bolshevik government came out with a Decree on Peace calling for immediate peace 'without annexations and indemnities'. The imperialist powers were engaged in a bloody conflict that, irrespective of which side was victorious, could only mean enslavement of peoples of colonies:

> The government considers it the greatest of crimes against humanity to continue this war over the issue of how to divide among the strong and rich nations the weak nationalities they have conquered, and solemnly announces its determination immediately to sign terms of peace to stop this war.

The decree then went on to announce that the nefarious designs of the imperialist powers would be made public by publishing secret treaties and agreements that the Tsarist and Lvov/Kerensky regimes had entered into for territorial gains. The Bolshevik government undertook to do away with secret diplomacy in its dealings with foreign states. Much to the consternation and embarrassment of the belligerents, Russia proceeded to publish the secret treaties forthwith (10 November onwards) initially in *Izvestia* and *Pravda*, and subsequently in a series of volumes of which seven were published between December 1917 and February 1918.

What impressed the nationalists most was the genuine commitment that the Bolsheviks had to national self-determination. Its commitment was demonstrated by the urgency with which Finland was granted independence in December 1917. This was in pursuance of the Declaration of the Rights of People of Russia (15 November 1917). The declaration was a charter for the liberation of oppressed nationalities. It enunciated the following basic principles:

> 1. Equality and sovereignty of the peoples of Russia.
> 2. The Right of the peoples of Russia to self-determination up to secession and the formation of an independent state.
> 3. Abrogation of all national and national-religious privileges and restrictions.
> 4. The free development of the national minorities and ethnographic groups inhabiting the territory of Russia.

This was a radical departure not just from the policies of the Tsarist state but policies also of western powers generally. It was greeted with immense fervour and hope by people fighting for freedom from colonial rule. We need to bear in mind that censorship and war conditions, combined with the massive misinformation campaign against the Bolsheviks, often prevented detailed or accurate news about developments in Russia from circulating in India. Nevertheless what could not be concealed was that a huge upheaval had occurred in the vast empire ruled over by a powerful Tsar, that the monarchy had been overthrown, that for the first time in history the rule of workers and peasants had been established, and that this was a state that would directly as well as through its example strengthen the struggle of the oppressed people of colonies. Moreover, a large amount of material circulated underground, keeping nationalist circles informed about what was happening in Russia. A lot of this material reached India through networks of Indian revolutionaries in different parts of the world. These networks were particularly active during the period of the war, operating from locations in Germany, Canada, USA, Afghanistan, Japan and London itself. Many of the left-wing and radical revolutionaries living abroad quickly turned towards Russia after November 1917.

Already in December 1915 a 'Provisional Government of Free India' had been formed by nationalists in Kabul, with Raja Mahendra Pratap Singh as president, Barkatulla as prime minister and a cabinet that included Obeidullah Sindhi. The provisional government had the support of a section of Afghan authorities, mainly those loyal to the crown prince, Amanullah Khan who was opposed to the commanding influence that the British had over Afghanistan. The pro-British ruler of Afghanistan, Habibullah Khan was assassinated in February 1919 and shortly afterwards Amanullah Khan became the ruler of Afghanistan. This precipitated a brief war with Britain (Third Anglo-Afghan War, 1919). The outcome of the war was that the British recognized Afghanistan as an independent state. Henceforth, Afghanistan under Amanullah became an ally of Bolshevik Russia. This had important implications for the nationalists based in Kabul. Amanullah's support for the provisional government headed by Raja Mahendra Pratap Singh had facilitated regular contact between Russia and the Indian government-in-exile. Mahendra Pratap Singh visited Petrograd in March 1918. The following year Barkatulla travelled to Moscow where he met Russian leaders. *Izvestia* published an interview with him. Then in May 1919 a delegation led by Mahendra Pratap Singh met Lenin at the Kremlin in Moscow. Reminiscing about this meeting Mahendra Pratap recalled vividly the warmth with which the delegation was received by Lenin:

> We entered a big room with a big table at which was sitting the famous Red Leader Comrade Lenin. I being at the head of the party entered first and proceeded towards the figure sitting right before me. To my astonishment the man or the hero stood up suddenly, went to a corner and fetched a small chair and put the chair near his office chair. And as I arrived by his side he asked me to sit down. For a moment I thought in my mind, where to sit, asking myself, should I sit on this small chair brought by Mr. Lenin himself or should I sit on one of the huge easy chairs covered with Morocco leather. I decided to sit on that small

> chair and sat down, while my friends, Moulana Barkatulla and others, took their seats on richly upholstered chairs. Comrade Lenin asked me, in what language he was to address me – English, French, German or Russian. I told him that we should better speak in English. And I presented to him my book *Religion of Love*. To my astonishment he said that he had already read it. Quickly arguing in my mind I could see that the pamphlets demanded by the Foreign Office a day earlier were meant for Lenin himself. Mr. Lenin said that my book was 'Tolstoyism'. I presented to him also my plan of having notes repayable not in gold or silver but in more necessary commodities such as wheat, rice, butter, oil, coal, etc. We had quite a long conversation.

Meanwhile, another group living in self-exile in Europe was active in the cause of freedom. This comprised nationalists who were based in Germany, mainly operating from Berlin. The leading figure of this group was Virendranath Chattopadhyay. In 1915 Chattopadhyay and his associates had established an Indian Independence Committee. Barkatulla, who later shifted to Kabul, and Har Dayal, were part of this initiative. The German government provided some logistical assistance to the Committee. After the October Revolution, Chattopadhyay and several other members of the Berlin group established contacts with Russia, and at the same time came under the influence of Marxism. In 1919 the Indian Independence Committee was dissolved, though the activities of the Berlin group did not cease. For Chattopadhyay, links with the Bolsheviks became increasingly crucial for nationalist activity.

The ideological shift towards Marxism, of left-wing revolutionary groups based in Afghanistan, Germany and elsewhere, saw expression in the formation of the Communist Party of India in October 1920 at Tashkent (which was at that time the capital of the Turkestan Autonomous Soviet Socialist Republic). One might mention that there was another ideological trend among groups working abroad, one that articulated opposition to British rule in terms of religious identity (Hindu nationalism; Pan-Islamism). This trend was reflected in the growth of communal politics and the promotion of divisive agendas in the 1920s in India. In turn this politics undermined the unity of the anti-colonial struggle. In the post-war years émigré groups and individuals representing this trend quickly distanced themselves from the communists even though they claimed to be working for the nationalist cause.

At the end of the war several thousand *muhajirs* who opted to live in exile to protest against Britain's role in dismantling the Ottoman Empire, had travelled to Afghanistan swelling the ranks of nationalist émigrés in that country – now ruled by Amanullah Khan whose hostility to the British we have already noted. A section of the *muhajirs* had become ardent champions of the socialist cause which, they were convinced, was the way forward for India. Some of these émigrés, of whom Mohammad Shafiq was perhaps the most prominent, proceeded to Tashkent where they joined other communists such as M.N. Roy and Abani Mukherjee in an endeavour to establish the Communist Party of India. Their organizational efforts at Tashkent were coordinated by the Comintern. The decisions of the Second Congress of Comintern (1920), to which reference has been made earlier, had provided the stimulus for such an initiative.

While discussing the antecedents of the new phase of the anti-colonial struggle in India under the impact of the October Revolution we need to make a special reference to the Ghadar revolutionaries. As is well known, the Ghadar Party was founded by nationalists in San Francisco (California) in 1913, under the leadership of Sohan Singh Bhakna. Within a short time the Ghadarites were able to extend the scope of their activities to Indian migrant labour in Canada, the Caribbean,

Philippines and Singapore. The Ghadarites linked the struggle against inhuman conditions in which Indian migrants in North America and Southeast Asia had to work, and the racial discrimination they faced, to the larger struggle against colonial rule and for the liberation of India. As a result of the infamous *Komagatamaru* episode of 1914, in which the Canadian authorities demonstrated their racial bigotry by denying entry to passengers aboard the ship when it reached Vancouver after a long and arduous journey from Hong Kong, and the violence unleashed against the passengers by British authorities at Budge Budge when the *Komagatamaru* arrived in India upon being forced to return from Canada, the Ghadar movement acquired a militant character. With the outbreak of the war the Ghadarites intensified their activities in several parts of the Indian subcontinent, especially among peasants in Punjab. In Punjab they strove to undermine the authority of the British raj, making it difficult for colonial officials to recruit soldiers in the province. Attempts were made to rally Indian soldiers (of whom a very large proportion was recruited from Punjab) for a mutiny in the British Indian armed forces. The plan did not succeed and provided the pretext for brutal repression of the Ghadarites. The Defence of India Act of 1915 was a legislative measure directed mainly against the Ghadarites. About fifty Ghadarites were executed, while several more were sentenced to transportation for life, or sentenced to life-imprisonment. The martyrdom of Kartar Singh Sarabha, who was barely nineteen years old when he was executed in 1915 was to inspire an entire generation of young revolutionaries of whom Bhagat Singh was the most prominent. Many of the leading Ghadarites became part of the communist movement after the October Revolution. The 1915 Act was used to incarcerate large numbers of revolutionaries for several years without trial. This was the prelude to the

Rowlatt Satyagraha and the Jallianwala Bagh Massacre. The post-war mass upsurge, and Gandhian mobilization from 1919 onwards, occurred in this political context. The Non-Cooperation Movement did not take place in a vacuum.

While on the one hand the British attempted to put the brakes on the radicalization of the nationalist movement by offering some minor concessions in the form of the Montagu – Chelmsford proposals and the Government of India Act of 1919, on the other hand they widened the scope of the Defence of India Act of 1915 through the more draconian and stringent provisions of the Anarchical and Revolutionary Crimes Act (Act XI of 1919), better known as the Rowlatt Act. This is how Indians were rewarded for their outstanding (albeit largely involuntary) contribution to the Allied victory in the First World War. It needs to be underlined that the main objective of the act, and of the continuing repressive measures to stamp out 'revolutionary crimes' (the wording of the title of the act is significant), was to restrain the rising tide of popular resistance and revolutionary mobilization. This, however, was no longer possible. Massive participation in the anti-Rowlatt agitation launched towards the end of March 1919 was a reflection of the anger which the act had aroused. More importantly such participation clearly showed that conditions were now ripe for mass mobilization against British rule. The hartal of 6 April 1919 was a huge success. Punjab was the epicentre of the agitation where Amritsar, Lahore and Gujranwala were the key locations of the agitation. The horrific massacre at Jallianwala Bagh on 13 April cannot be attributed merely to the aberrant personal conduct of Reginald Dyer. It was very much part of the brutally repressive regime that had been imposed on Punjab during the war, and the relentless persecution of Ghadarite and other revolutionaries. Jallianwala Bagh was meant to be a lesson to opponents of

British authority. Historically it is immaterial whether it was an individual decision or had the general sanction of Dyer's superiors. The entire colonial machinery was complicit in the massacre, as was made more than apparent by the exoneration of Dyer and the endorsement of his action in white racist circles. What could have been a better illustration of this than the provocative gesture of collecting nearly £27,000 to be given to the 'butcher of Amritsar' by way of felicitating him?

The anti-Rowlatt agitation and the wave of popular unrest that followed the Jallianwala Bagh massacre ushered in an era of mass mobilization against colonial rule. It goes without saying that Gandhi played a major role hereafter in shaping the national movement, and leading it for the next two decades. Nevertheless, standard nationalist historiography has tended to downplay or ignore the fact that the ground had already been prepared in the preceding years for the political shift, involving mass participation and novel forms of protest, which occurred from 1919 onwards. The radical and popular thrust which the anti-colonial struggle acquired due to the impact of the October Revolution made such a shift almost inevitable. Moreover, satyagraha in its strictest Gandhian sense, which required the satyagrahi to have accumulated considerable spiritual and moral strength, was only one of the several methods adopted by people. More militant methods too were resorted to. For instance R. K. Das in his pioneering *Factory Labour in India* (Berlin, 1923) lists a series of industrial strikes in 1919 and 1920 involving thousands of workers: 35,000 jute workers in Calcutta; general strike by two lakh workers in Bombay in January 1920; strike by 25,000 mill workers in Ahmedabad; strike by 60,000 mill workers in Bombay in the third week of March 1920, to mention a few examples. The All India Trade Union Congress (AITUC) held its inaugural session at Bombay in October 1920. Lala Lajpat Rai presided over the session and several nationalist leaders including Motilal Nehru and Annie Besant were among those who attended. Within a few years communists established their hold over AITUC.

The Non-Cooperation Movement of 1920-22 was indeed a huge mass movement. Gandhi was both its architect and foremost leader. The movement was unprecedented in its scope, and had an all-India spread. By 1921 it gained a momentum of its own. Peasants were drawn into the movement in large numbers transforming the movement into a fight against landlordism. Communities dependent upon forest produce for their daily subsistence took to incendiarism to register their protest against colonial policies, as happened in Uttarakhand. Militant trade union action in Calcutta saw the emergence of a group of dedicated communists in the city during 1921-22. Muzaffar Ahmad played a leading role in this process, which marked the beginning of his life as a great communist revolutionary. And in Malabar the struggle of the Mappila tenants for their rights, against the backdrop of the Non-Cooperation Movement, acquired a violent character. Communal historiography has invariably presented the Mappila uprising in terms of a religious conflict, in which Mappila peasants are demonized, and this version continues to be a favourite theme in communal propaganda. Gandhi and sections of the nationalist leadership were getting worried by late 1921 about the radical nature that the Non-Cooperation Movement had assumed in several parts of the country, especially among dispossessed sections of society. Consequently the abrupt suspension of the movement in February 1922 due to the violent incidents at Chauri Chaura was not really unexpected. But it did cause widespread demoralization.

This demoralization prompted a leftward shift among several sections of nationalists after 1922. The experience of the October Revolution in Russia and the excitement over the revolutionary initiatives of the Bolsheviks attracted an increasing number of activists to socialist ideas and communism. At the same time there were many who took the path of communal politics, so that the communal situation became particularly serious in the later half of the 1920s. Gandhi had made the Khilafat issue the central issue of the Non-Cooperation Movement. Though this remains a matter of debate, it is undeniable that the choice of the issue was perhaps somewhat inappropriate for this phase of the anticolonial struggle. It diluted the immense radical potential of the Non-Cooperation Movement. The Khilafat problem, as distinct from the larger question of Turkish independence and imperialist territorial aggrandizement in the erstwhile Ottoman lands, was devoid of possibilities of progressive politics, as events in Turkey soon demonstrated. The Khilafat was abolished in 1924, thus making the problem irrelevant from the point of view of carrying forward the anti-colonial struggle. The implications of banking upon the emotive appeal of what was essentially a religious issue, for mass mobilization became clear soon after the Non-Cooperation Movement was withdrawn. As it is sections of nationalists both within and outside the Congress who had engaged in politics of religious identity, seeking to define the Indian nation in terms of the superior claim of 'Hindus' (regarded, as the colonial state did, in terms of a monolithic and homogeneous pan-Indian community) had not been enthusiastic about the Khilafat agitation, notwithstanding that Gandhi himself was genuinely committed to it. Unfortunately the constant reference to the need for 'Hindu-Muslim Unity' by leaders of the Khilafat agitation reinforced the notion, which the colonial state vigorously promoted, that the two communities, conceptualized as being internally undifferentiated, were inherently antagonistic to each other. The British were not entirely unhappy about the rapid growth of communal politics, and the state did not really have much interest in preventing riots and situations of conflict often over the most trivial issues, issues which were articulated in terms of some (usually imagined) religious grievance. The unintended long-term consequence of focussing on the Khilafat issue was the legitimization of such grievances. Communalism could always be used to disrupt the national movement.

It is not easy to assess the huge historical impact that a revolutionary upheaval of the magnitude of the October Revolution in Russia has had on the course of history, or even specifically on the course of Indian history. A century might not be adequate for such an assessment, the more so as Russia has itself disowned, at least officially, the Great October Revolution and erased nearly seventy-five years of its history. The superhuman sacrifices of the Soviet people, especially during the Second World War, to rescue the world from fascism and Nazism, have been shamefully repudiated not just by Russia and most of the constituents of pre-dissolution USSR, but by regimes extending from Poland to the Czech Republic which were liberated with the assistance of the Soviet Red Army. Yet, in the words of E. J. Hobsbawm, 'There is no way in which the Soviet era can be written out of Russian or world history, as though it had not been. There is no way in which St Petersburg can return to 1914' (*The Age of Extremes: 1914-1991*).

PART II

THE FALL

'History may make a clean sweep, but fears emptiness'

Bertolt Brecht, 1954

SEVENTY GLORIOUS YEARS: ACHIEVEMENTS AND PROBLEMS (1987)

B. T. Ranadive

The seventy years after the Great October Socialist Revolution, the first breach in the world capitalist order, have been years of explosive changes and world transformations. These were made possible because of the mighty success of the Soviet people in socialist planning, the first conduct of the policy of peace and peaceful coexistence, assurance of complete equality to all the nationalities and peoples inhabiting the Soviet Union, the unparalleled sacrifices of the Soviet men and women in the anti-fascist war to save their country and humanity from fascist bondage, and the great military skill of Soviet leaders and the heroism of the Soviet soldiers.

These transformatory successes include the socialist revolution in one-third of the world, smashing of the old colonial order liberating enslaved nations, along with the successes of the dictatorship of the proletariat in the Soviet Union guided by the science of Marxism-Leninism, practised by the Marxist-Leninist Party, the CPSU.

In his article on the 4th Anniversary of the October Revolution Lenin wrote,

> But we have right to be and are proud that to us has fallen the good fortune to *begin* the building of Soviet state, and thereby to *usher* in a new era in world history, the era of the rule of a *new* class, a class which is oppressed in every capitalist country, but which everywhere is marching forward towards a new life, towards victory over the bourgeoisie, towards the dictatorship of the proletariat, towards the emancipation of mankind from the yoke of capital and from imperialist wars.[1]

[1] V. I. Lenin, *Collected Works*, Vol. 33, p. 55.

The seventy years following the October Revolution have witnessed a growing fulfilment of what Lenin wrote.

Single-handedly the Soviet people had to fight the problems arising on the morrow of the Great October Revolution. Building of socialism in a backward country was an unchartered sea. The eagle eye vision of Lenin saw the difficulties, anticipated the twists and turns and indicated the correct path. After his death the responsibility for this unique and unparalleled task fell on the shoulders of the Bolshevik Party headed by Stalin. The Leninist guidance and teachings and faithful adherence to them, enabled the Party to discharge its historic task and tremendously accelerate the world revolutionary process.

IDEOLOGICAL CONSOLIDATION

At each stage the leadership of the Bolshevik Party had to wage a bitter struggle for a correct policy of advance based on Lenin's teachings and guidance. The inner and bitter controversies inside the Party were waged between those who followed Lenin's teachings and those who questioned their correctness. It was vital for the new working class state that these controversies were resolved correctly otherwise its very existence would have been endangered.

The deviationists sought to disarm the victorious working class of the Soviet Union by calling upon its Party to give up the idea of building socialism in the Soviet Union, holding that it cannot be done in a single country. A powerful section of Bolshevik leaders, among them Trotsky, fought for this anti-Leninist, anti-revolutionary stand. If the majority of the Party had succumbed to the erroneous and reactionary counsel, revolution would have lost its capacity to defend itself, against the attacks of the imperialist powers and internal reactionary forces. It would have been economically and militarily completely crippled.

But the Party headed by Stalin, who was foremost in defending Leninist guidance rejected these deviationist counsels and upheld the Leninist course.

> Uneven economic and political development is an absolute law of capitalism. Hence the victory of socialism is possible first in several or even in one capitalist country taken separately. The victorious proletariat of that country, having expropriated the capitalists and *organized its own socialist production* would stand-up against the rest of the world, the capitalist world, attracting to its cause the oppressed classes of the other countries, raising revolts in those countries against the capitalists, and in the event of necessity coming out with armed force against the exploiting class and their state.[2]

This Leninist decision and the subsequent drawing up of the first five-year plan must be considered to be the turning point in the development and consolidation of the revolution. This was to decide in the next few years not only the fate of the proletarian state, but also played a vital role in giving a blow to imperialist encirclement and unleashed new revolutionary forces in the world.

The CPSU and the Soviet Union were the first to introduce socialist planning and put into practice a planned economy. For the capitalist world it was not only a novel idea, it was an unworkable fantasy. The eyes of all people, the oppressed as well as the oppressors, were focused on the developments in the Soviet Union. It was realised that it was a question of struggle between two social systems. The successes of the first

[2] Lenin, *Collected Works*, Vol. 21 pp. 232-33.

five-year plan were a gigantic victory for the socialist economy and production, scored by the state of the working class, the dictatorship of the proletariat, and the CPSU. They declared the supremacy of the socialist system over the capitalist system. The imperialists from now had to face not an economically backward country but a powerful, modern, economically united country capable of looking after its own defence.

Summing up of the first five year plan, the Report delivered by Stalin to the joint Plenum of the Central Committee and the Central Control Commission of the CPSU (B) in January 1933 said,

> The results of the first five-year plan have shattered the thesis of the social democrats that it is impossible to build socialism in one country taken separately. The results of the first five year plan have shown that it is quite possible to build a socialist society in one country; for the economic foundations of such a society have already been laid in the USSR.
>
> The results of the first five-year plan have refuted the assertion of bourgeois economists that the capitalist system of economy is the best of all systems, that every other system of economy is unstable and incapable of standing the test of the difficulties of economic development. The results of the five year plan have shown that the capitalist system of economy is bankrupt and unstable; that it has outlived its day and must give way to another, a higher, Soviet, socialist system of economy; that the only system of economy that has no fear of crises and is able to overcome the difficulties which capitalism cannot solve, is the Soviet system of economy.[3]

Those who considered that socialism could not be built in a single country especially in a backward country like Russia

[3] J.V. Stalin, *Works*, Vol. 13, p. 219.

were in effect underestimating the revolutionary role of the peasantry and of the workers and peasants led by the working class. This underestimation was again seen when they raised a controversy inside the Party on the question of alliance with the middle peasants. Once again a majority of the Party headed by Stalin had to fight against the deviation and defeat it. An error on the question of the peasantry would again have ruined the chances of building socialism and compromized the very existence of the working class state. In fact, these opportunist elements forgot what Lenin wrote about the dictatorship of the proletariat in Russia when he described it as a special type of alliance between the peasantry, petty-bourgeoisie, etc., and the working class, under the leadership of the working class for the achievement of socialism. Similar differences arose over the question of collectivization of agriculture and the fight against the kulaks as a class. Without overcoming the resistance of the kulaks, the capitalist elements in the rural areas, there was no chance of taking the rural areas forward, to collective farming and making them a component part of building socialism.

It is by defeating the left and right deviations inside the Party that the CPSU and the working class state were able to ensure a consistent march to a new society, towards socialism. These battles immediately after the establishment of proletarian rule played a vital role in keeping the policies of the Soviet state on the correct Leninist path.

VICTORY OVER FASCISM

The struggle for socialist planning and transformation was immensely helped by the policies on the national question of the Soviet state, which assured complete equality to all nationalities residing in the Soviet Union and removal of all earlier oppression under the Tsarist regime. This policy also ensured that the masses of different nationalities could be liberated in only by the proletarian state, which was based on the ending of exploitation of backward nationalities from the yoke of feudal landlords.

The success of the five-year plan was helped by the successful struggle for international peace and proletarian internationalism waged by the proletarian state. The historic decree on peace drafted by Lenin and adopted by the Soviet government constituted a new development in international relations and underlined the proletarian way of solving international problems. The Decree on Peace said,

> The workers' and peasants' government created by the Revolution of 24-25 October and basing itself on the Soviets of Workers' and Peasants' Deputies, calls upon all the belligerent people and their governments to start immediate negotiations for a just, democratic peace . . . by such a peace the government means an immediate peace without annexations (that is, without the seizure of foreign lands, without the forcible incorporation of foreign nations) and without indemnities.[4]

The imperialist war of 1914-18 was fought precisely for annexations, seizure of territories and colonies. The Soviet declaration for peace introduced a new era of equality and freedom among the nations of the world consistent with the international outlook of the successful revolution. Since then the world has seen a continuous fight waged by the Soviet state, the dictatorship of the proletariat, in the interests of peace, against annexations and war, and for the liberations of all the enslaved nations. The Soviet state and the CPSU firmly adhere to the policy of peaceful coexistence between states having different social systems.

[4] Lenin, *Collected Works*, Vol. 26, p. 249.

The Soviet state could successfully rally the forces of democracy and peace in the struggle against the fascist war menace in the 1930s. The imperialist powers, Britain, France and others were begging Hitler to attack the Soviet Union. Hitler himself had declared his intention to expand the territorial frontiers of Germany at the expense of the USSR. The Soviet proposals for collective security to check Hitler and avoid war were repeatedly opposed by the imperialist governments of Britain and France and were sabotaged by the reformist democratic leaders of Germany, France and Britain. The appeasement policy pursued by these governments inevitably led to war among the imperialists and later on against the Soviet Union. The world had to pay an enormous price in millions of lives to save itself from bondage from fascism, to protect its liberty. The anti-Soviet line of the imperialists only succeeded in jeopardizing the liberties of all nations.

The imperialist governments and countries collapsed before the Nazi attacks. The Soviet Union, the only socialist state at that time, bore the brunt of the Nazi attack and broke the back of Nazi Germany. As many as 20 million out of a total of 50 million who died in the war, were sons and daughters of the Soviet Union. The Hitlerite Nazis could not stand against this invincible combination of patriotism and socialism, the combination of defence of the motherland with loyalty and proletarian internationalism. The Soviet people and the Soviet state covered themselves with imperishable glory. This historic victory of the Soviet Union was the second most important event in world history after the Great October Socialist Revolution. It led to the emergence of a number of socialist states in Eastern Europe, facilitated the achievement of independence by India, paved the way for the success of the Great Chinese Revolution and successful revolutions in Vietnam, Korea and later on in Cuba. It gave a blow to the old colonial order and changed the balance of class forces in the world.

The liberationist role of the war was announced in Stalin's address to the Soviet people over Moscow Radio explaining the line of the Central Committee of the CPSU. Stalin said,

> The war with fascist Germany cannot be considered an ordinary war, it is not only a war between two armies, it is also Great War of the Soviet people against the German fascist army. The aim of this people's patriotic war against the fascist oppressors is not only to avert the danger that is hanging over our country, but also to aid all European peoples who are groaning under the yoke of German fascism. In this war of liberation we shall not be alone. In this great war we shall have true allies in the peoples of Europe and America, including the German people which is enslaved by the Hitlerite misrulers. Our war for the freedom of our motherland will merge with the struggle of the peoples of Europe and America for independence, for democratic liberties. It will be a united front of the peoples, who stand for freedom and against enslavement by Hitler's fascist armies.

The total transformatory character of the anti-fascist victory was summed up by a meeting of the communists' and workers' parties in 1957, when it characterized the post-victory period as a new epoch of transition from capitalism to socialism, an epoch when the international socialist system is becoming the decisive factor determining the course of world development, an epoch of national liberation and socialist revolutions, of rapid decay and disintegration of colonialism, an epoch of the collapse of imperialism and the final victory of socialism and communism on a world scale. This sums up the grand success of Marxism-Leninism and the CPSU's line, a success scored under the dictatorship of the proletariat.

CONSOLIDATION OF SOCIALISM

The four decades since the gigantic victory have been decades of constant struggle, advanced and continuous fight against the imperialists and their global designs especially of the US imperialists. The US imperialists have been planning for a war against socialist countries since the end of the anti-fascist war itself. The efforts of the imperialists to set the clock back have failed, though they continue to hatch new conspiracies. The years since the anti-fascist victory have seen the consistent initiative of the Soviet Union in the interests of struggling people, checkmating imperialist plans of neo-colonialist aggression and expansion. Gone are the days when the imperialists could decide unilaterally the fate of peoples and nations. The Soviet Union helped Afghanistan to maintain its independence; its aid to the Arab people, to the peoples of Africa has been rendered possible because of the increased strength of socialism, of the power of the first socialist state. Socialism and the socialist camp have become a world power following the anti-fascist victory of the Soviet Union.

The change in the balance of forces has helped newly liberated countries to maintain their independence and pursuit of a foreign policy of non-alignment. The consistent pursuit of this policy by many countries, especially India, tilts the world balance in favour of peace, democracy and socialism and obstructs the designs of imperialist war-mongers.

The increasing strength of the socialist economy of the Soviet Union and the advance of other socialist countries help in guarding and maintaining the economic independence and self-reliance of many newly liberated countries. But for this help the economies of many newly liberated countries would have been helplessly dependent on Western aid. India has greatly benefited from timely Soviet help to rear her vital public sector in strategic industries, without which she would have had to seek the help of imperialists who were from the very beginning opposed to the public sector and strategic industries in India. It is not accidental that almost all public sector concerns in the strategic industries, steel, oil, machinery and vital defence production were built with the help of the Soviet Union and other socialist countries.

Indo-Soviet cooperation extending over decades stands witness to this world role of the socialist economy. In the case of India, the Indo-Soviet Treaty of Friendship, Cooperation and Peace is of great importance in strengthening the security of the country and maintaining stability in the sub-continent. But for this Treaty, and the all round help in economic and defence fields, India's position would have been precarious in the face of the continuous and constant pouring in of arms by the U.S. imperialists into Pakistan.

The socialist system once again displayed its complete superiority over the capitalist system in the post-war rehabilitation period. Countries of Western Europe, reeling under the destruction and havoc caused because of the war, took a long time to recover. Many of them had to depend on help from the USA which had escaped war destruction and prospered during the war. But the Soviet Union, suffering from colossal devastation and destruction of its productive powers, single-handedly restored its economy in the shortest possible time. The imperialist bourgeoisie and their press had estimated that it would take the Soviet Union decades to rebuild its war-ravaged economy and that American help would be needed. They were to be disappointed.

In March 1946, within less than a year of the end of the war, the USSR Supreme Soviet adopted a plan for the reconstruction and development of the USSR economy for the years 1946-50. The target of the plan was to attain the pre-war level of industrial and agricultural development and gradually to surpass it. The socialist system functioning under the dictatorship of the proletariat and the leadership of the Marxist-Leninist party was able to rouse the enthusiasm of millions of workers in this task.

But this was not enough to meet the needs of the socialist economy. It was, therefore, followed by widespread socialist competition to surpass the 4th five-year plan target. The pre-war industrial levels were surpassed by 1948, after only two and a half years. Since then the Soviet economy has registered one spectacular advance after another, despite having to face some difficulties.

These successes were not achieved without serious mistakes on the part of those who ran the proletarian state, on the part of the party which guided the socialist society, and without ideological deviations from Leninist norms.

In his article on the 4th Anniversary of the October Revolution Lenin wrote,

> The Soviet system is one of the most vivid proofs, or manifestations, of how the one revolution develops into the other. The Soviet system provides the maximum of democracy for the workers and peasants; at the same time it marks a break with *bourgeois* democracy and the rise of a *new*, epoch-making *type* of democracy, namely proletarian democracy, or the dictatorship of the proletariat.
>
> Let the curs and swine of the moribund bourgeoisie and the petty-bourgeois democrats who trail behind them heap imprecations, abuse and derision upon our heads for our reverses and mistakes in the work of building up *our* Soviet system. We do not forget for a moment that we have committed and are committing numerous mistakes and are suffering numerous reverses. How can reverses and mistakes be avoided in a matter so new in the history of the world as the building of an unprecedented *type* of state edifice! We shall work steadfastly to set our reverses and mistakes right and to improve our practical

application of Soviet principles, which is still very, very far from being perfect.[5]

SHORTCOMINGS AND ERRORS

The mistakes arising from the personality cult of Stalin, the harm it did by slowing down further progress, the bureaucratism and other evils, were fought and rectified, showing the vitality of the Marxist-Leninist party, the Soviet party. Notwithstanding these mistakes, there have been gigantic achievements and progress. Without such progress and advance it would not have been possible to defeat Hitler and rebuild the socialist economy and bring it to the forefront of the world in economic and social advance.

Notwithstanding these achievements, the shortcomings and errors in the functioning of the dictatorship of the proletariat, the ideological errors should be noted. Some of these errors distort the functioning of the proletarian state. Their source and origin must be properly understood. The violations of socialist democracy under Stalin's leadership require an objective analysis. This is not to bypass or neglect mistakes which can be traced directly to Stalin and his policies. The question is why such violations should occur under the state of the dictatorship of the proletariat which guarantees democracy for the millions, for the mass of the people. The Soviet Union was the first experience of running the dictatorship of the proletariat. It was a voyage on unchartered seas and mistakes were bound to occur. The working class, taking the reigns of power for the first time in history, (the experience of the Paris Commune was short-lived), and that too in a huge peasant-dominated country, had to run the state without previous experience or guidance. The conditions

[5] *Collected Works*, Vol. 33, pp. 54-55.

under which power was captured and the continuing resistance of the exploiting classes, helped from abroad, demanded strict punitive measures. It is now known that these were continued even when the situation ceased to warrant them.

This raises the question of the guarantees of individual liberty under proletarian rule. It was here that previous guidance and experience was lacking. Marx, Engels and Lenin had outlined in detail the *class* relationship under the dictatorship of the proletariat. In general it was also stated that proletarian dictatorship meant democracy for the mass of the people, for 98 per cent of the people. Marx analysed the experience of the Paris Commune, but the question of the relationship between the individual from the class – the individual from the toiling masses – and the dictatorship of the class had not figured in the discussion. It was believed that once the regime of the exploiting classes was overthrown, the working class and toilers would hardly have any problems of democratic rights in relation to their own state. This proved to be wrong. Abolition of the rule of exploiters does not end the need of guaranteed rights by the state; the need continues till the end. This has to be ideologically understood and worked out. The failure to understand this led to a number of the distortions in the functioning of the dictatorship of the proletariat.

In the earlier years, whenever the question of individual rights was raised, whenever it was suggested that freedom of the individual was restricted under the state of the dictatorship of the proletariat – the answer used to be that freedom from exploitation was the highest freedom, and the individuals possessed this freedom under the state of proletariat. In addition it was stated that the freedom of the individual under the bourgeois state was only a formal freedom in the absence of freedom from exploitation. Thus, freedom of the individual was completely identified with freedom from exploitation. It was not realised that freedom from exploitation alone was not enough guarantee to protect the individual from the maladministration of the state.

There are a number of reasons for this. In the first place the historic heritage of the dictatorship of the proletariat was underestimated. Secondly the main instrument which was to provide the proletarian state with guarantees of individual rights of freedom showed inner weaknesses.

In discussing the malfunctioning of the proletarian state we must demarcate ourselves from the usual rabid criticism coming from imperialist and bourgeois quarters. They have been denouncing the proletarian state as a totalitarian dictatorship of the same type as any fascist state. Their main attack has been on the lack of individual freedom under these regimes, but their real target was the socialization of the means of production.

These critiques naturally present a distorted picture, only highlighting the mistakes under the leadership of Stalin. They deliberately conceal the monumental achievements under his leadership – abolition of exploitation, the rearing of a socialist society, freedom from poverty, unemployment, economic crisis, and the success of the socialist plans which in the shortest possible time industrialized a backward agrarian country. Backed by these achievements the USSR was not only able to defeat the marauding forces of Hitler but achieved new economic successes one after another, registering a steady growth of national income when the capitalist world was shaken by a widespread economic crisis. Other socialist countries have been making similar progress guided by their socialist states.

SOURCE OF MISTAKES

The question however is what was the source of mistakes during Stalin's leadership – mistakes in the functioning of the state, of violations of socialist democracy and liberty of the individual.

In the first place it seems that Lenin's warning against the heritage, the character of the state inherited from the past was ignored, so also was his warning that the state would not be properly run unless there was sufficient 'culture' to assert, unless the proletariat acquires this culture; his warnings against the rapid growth of bureaucracy and use of violence and organizational methods were also treated lightly.

The bureaucracy is a bourgeois-landlord institution incompatible with proletarian democracy. Bureaucrats and people appointed by them cannot run a proletarian machine. So long as such people run the state and the government, constitutional and basic guarantees are required against misuse of power by individuals, officials, against violation of the rights of the ordinary citizen.

It should have been obvious that the new proletarian state was being run by people emerging out of the old society; that petty-bourgeois and bourgeois habits would continue for a long time; and bureaucratism in running the state would remain; there would be tendency to erode the right of dissent and the liberties of the individual. The proletarian state had precisely to address itself to these problems after the suppression of internal enemies. Unfortunately this was not done. The question of individual liberty, of the relationship of the individual to the proletarian state was considered as solved after the establishment of class liberty.

Writing in January 1923, Lenin saw the problem of heritage of the past thus,

> With the exception of the People's Commissariat of Foreign Affairs, our state apparatus is to a considerable extent a survival of the past and has hardly undergone any serious change. It has only been slightly touched up on the surface, but in all other respects it is most typical relic of our state machine. And so, to find a method of reality renovating it, I think we ought to turn for experience to our Civil War. How did we act in the more critical moments of the Civil War? We concentrated our best Party forces in the Red Army; we mobilized the best of our workers; we looked for new forces at the deepest roots of our dictatorship.[6]

Only the best working class elements inspired by the spirit of revolution, and devotion to its cause, could tackle the bureaucratic heritage of the past.

Lenin had referred to the same topic in 1922,

> We inherited it, in effect, from the old regime, for it was absolutely impossible to reorganize it in such a short time, especially in conditions of war, famine, etc. That is why those 'critics' who point to the defects of our administrative machinery out of mockery or malice, may be calmly answered that they do not in the least understand the conditions of the revolution today. It is altogether impossible in five years to reorganize the machinery adequately, especially in the conditions in which our revolution took place. It is enough that in five years we have created a new type of state in which the workers are leading the peasantry against the bourgeoisie; and in a hostile international environment this in itself is a gigantic achievement. But knowledge of this must on no account blind us to the fact that, in effect, we took over the old machinery of state from the Tsar and the bourgeoisie and that now, with the onset of

[6] *Collected Works*, Vol. 33 p. 481.

> peace and satisfaction of the minimum requirements against famine, all our work must be directed towards improving the administrative machinery.[7]

Once again the same remedy is proposed – draw in workers untouched by bureaucraticism and firmly loyal and belonging to the lower stratum.

> I think that a few dozen workers, being members of the C.C. can deal better than anybody else with checking, improving and remodelling our state apparatus .... In my opinion, the workers admitted to the Central Committee should come preferably not from those who have had long service in Soviet bodies ... because those workers have already acquired the very traditions and the very prejudices which it is desirable to combat. The working class members of the C.C. must be mainly workers of a lower stratum than those promoted in the last five years to work in Soviet bodies; they must be people closer to being rank and file workers and peasants, who, however do not fall into the category of direct or indirect exploiters.[8]

Lenin saw aristocrats and bureaucrats developing in the administration especially in connection with the treatment of smaller nationalities,

> From what I was told by Comrade Dzerzhinsky, who was at the head of the commission sent by the C.C. to 'investigate' the Georgian incident, I could only draw the greatest apprehensions. If matters had come to such a pass that Orjonikidze could go to the extent of applying physical violence, as Comrade Dzerzhinsky informed me, we can imagine what a mess we

[7] *Collected Works*, Vol. 36, pp. 596-97.
[8] *Collected Works*, Vol. 36, p. 597.

have got ourselves into . . . . I think that Stalin's haste and his infatuation with pure administration, together with his spite against the notorious 'nationalist-socialism' played a fatal role here. In politics spite generally plays the basest of roles . . . And, to tell the truth, those nationalist-socialists were citizens who were accused of a political crime, and the terms of the accusation were such that it could not be described otherwise.[9]

Lenin laid his finger on the difficulties in building a new state, the human material, the lack of experience, the problem of heritage, and the lack of culture as he called it.

> The most harmful thing here would be haste. The most harmful thing would be to rely on the assumption that we know at least something, or that we have any considerable number of elements necessary for the building of a really new state apparatus, one really worthy to be called socialist, Soviet etc. No, we are ridiculously deficient of such an apparatus, and even of the elements of it, and we must remember that we should not stint time on building it, and that it will take many, many years.
>
> What elements have we for building the apparatus? Only two. First, the workers who are absorbed in the struggle for socialism. These elements are not sufficiently educated. They would like to build a better apparatus for us, but they do not know how. They cannot build one. They have not yet developed the culture required for this; and it is culture that is required. Nothing will be achieved in this by doing things in a rush, by assault, by whim or vigour, or in general, by any of the best human qualities. Secondly, we have elements of knowledge, education and training, but they are ridiculously inadequate compared with all other countries. Here we must not forget that we are too prone to compensate (or imagine that we can

[9] *Collected Works*, Vol. 36, p. 597.

compensate) our lack of knowledge by zeal, haste, etc.[10]

These were the difficulties of the first dictatorship of the proletariat to rear a state machine worthy of being called Soviet. As Lenin pointed out, the state machine did vanquish the exploiters, ensured the workers' and peasants' alliance. It was, however, unable to change the old apparatus completely.

This meant that a continuous running battle against the growth of bureaucracy, against the lack of 'culture' was required.

The pervading influence of bureaucracy in all spheres – government, party, cooperatives continued and were also taken note of by Stalin.

Addressing the 17th Congress of the CPSU (B) in 1934, i.e., a decade after Lenin warned against the growth of bureaucracy, Stalin said,

> What are the difficulties; and wherein are they lodged? They are difficulties attending in our organizational leadership. They are lodged in ourselves, in our leading people, in our organizations, in the apparatus of our party, state, economy, trade union, Young Communist League and all other organizations . . . . Bureaucracy and red tape in the administrative apparatus; idle chatter about 'leadership in general' instead of real and concrete leadership . . . The bureaucrats and red tapists have long become past masters in the art of demonstrating their loyalty to party and government decisions in words, and pigeon-holing them in deed.[11]

Notwithstanding this awareness, the growth of bureaucratism continued and increased, primarily in this

[10] *Collected Works*, Vol. 33, p. 488.
[11] *Problems of Leninism*, pp. 644-45.

period as subsequent events showed. It resulted, as it was bound to result, in the violation of norms of socialist democracy, violations of the rights of individuals, arbitrary arrests, trials and imprisonment of thousands of people. This went on for some years in the midst of new victories of the proletarian state on the economic front and the historic victory against the Nazi invaders.

This first bitter experience of dictatorship of the proletariat shows that abolition of economic exploitation did not *ipso facto* establish a proper relationship between the individual of the emancipated class and the state of the class. Arbitrariness with regard to the individual on the part of the state did not disappear automatically. It shows that a prolonged struggle was necessary to change the habits and outlook of the personnel of the administration and revealed that even under the proletarian state the constitution must contain built-in provisions against the arbitrary behaviour of the officials and others manning the administration. The general declaration of rights was not enough. There should be enough provisions in the constitution to guarantee them against the several arms of the government.

It seems that the problem was not properly understood for a long time. The attack against bureaucratism, directed in the earlier years (under Stalin) related to the failure of the executive to implement economic and other decisions of the government and the party, failure to execute policy decisions. It did not relate to the arbitrary arrests of individuals and their repression. So far as the rights of individuals were concerned, the problem was considered as settled since the exploiting state and exploiting classes were no longer there.

This is clearly seen from Stalin's otherwise brilliant speech explaining the Draft of the 1936 (Stalin) Constitution,

> Lastly, there is still one more specific feature of the Draft of

> the new constitution. Bourgeois constitutions usually confine themselves to stating the formal rights of citizens, without bothering about the conditions for the exercise of these rights, about the opportunity for exercising them, about the means by which they can be exercised . . . What distinguishes the draft of the new constitution is the fact that it does not confine itself to stating the formal rights of citizens, but especially stresses the guarantees of these rights, the means by which these rights can be exercised. *It does not merely proclaim equality of rights of citizens, but ensures it by giving legislative embodiment to the fact that the regime of exploitation has been abolished, to the fact that the citizens have been emancipated from all exploitation.* It does not merely proclaim the right to work but ensures it by giving legislative embodiment to the fact that there are no crisis in Soviet society, and that unemployment has been abolished. It does not merely proclaim democratic liberties, but legislatively ensures them by providing definite material resources. It is clear, therefore, that the democratism of the draft of the new constitution is not the 'ordinary' and 'universally recognized' democratism in the abstract, but 'socialist democratism'.[12]

The claims made here about the right to work, a freedom from exploitation and material resources for exercising the rights are certainly true. They constitute the great achievements of the proletarian state. But do they exhaust the question of democratic liberties, of the relationship between the individual and the state of his class? Do they *ipso facto* guarantee the individual against the arbitrary behaviour of state officials, when the existence of bureaucracy is admitted? Stalin only a year or two before this speech placed the problem of bureaucracy before the party and the people. But now in this speech he seems to be totally unaware of it. In fact,

[12] *Problems of Leninism*, pp. 692-693. Emphasis added.

this was the period when arbitrary acts and bureaucratism were reaching a new level in the USSR in the midst of the undoubted achievements of the Soviet state. And besides even though material resources for exercising the rights – public halls for exercising the right of meetings, etc., are placed in the hands of the class, the question of differing minorities in the class remains.

CHANGING PHASES OF DICTATORSHIP OF THE PROLETARIAT

It is of course obvious that there should be many restrictions on individual freedom immediately after the revolution. Without these the task of fighting the counter-revolution cannot be carried out successfully. Stalin correctly understood the changing phases of the dictatorship of the proletariat. Addressing the 18th Congress of the CPSU (B) in 1939, Stalin said,

> Since the October Revolution, our socialist state has passed through two main phases in it development. The first phase was the period from the October Revolution to the elimination of the exploiting classes. The principal task in that period was to suppress the resistance of the overthrown classes, to organize the defence of the country against the attack of the interventionists, to restore industry and agriculture, and to prepare the conditions for the elimination of the capitalist elements . . . . The second phase was the period from the elimination of the capitalist elements in town and country to the complete victory of the socialist economic system and the adoption of the new constitution. The principal task in this period was to establish the socialist economic system all over the country and to eliminate the last remnants of the capitalist elements, to organize a cultural revolution, and to organize a

> thoroughly modern army for the defence of the country .... The function of military suppression within the country ceased, died away; for exploitation had been abolished, there were no more exploiters left, and so there was no one to suppress. In place of this function of suppression, the state acquired the function of protecting socialist property from thieves and pilferers of the property of the people.[13]

It is strange that precisely when Stalin was saying that there was no class necessity for repression, serious violations of liberties were taking place. It once again showed that notwithstanding the end of class exploitation, the administration does not automatically function free from arbitrary behaviour and requires prolonged guarantees against such malfunctioning.

LEGAL PROVISIONS

The exposure of the cult of personality around Stalin did not lead to a proper understanding of the problem of individual liberty in the proletarian state, and the weaknesses revealed in the functioning of the dictatorship of the proletariat. It took more than two decades, nearly a quarter century, to realise that special provisions were necessary to protect individual liberty under the dictatorship of the proletariat. The 1977 constitution, for the first time introduced provisions for guaranteeing the liberty and freedom of the individual vis-à-vis the state. It was realised that neither repudiation of the concept of dictatorship of the proletariat nor describing the state as a state of whole people, could solve the problem.

If we examine the constitution of the USSR, some of the weaknesses become clear. The constitution of the USSR,

[13] Ibid., pp. 796-797.

since 1918, guarantees rights to the common man which no bourgeois constitution could think of. The right to work, the right to education, the freedom from exploitation, equality in relation to the means of production, the assurance of material means to implement these rights, all these are unprecedented rights which were never previously declared or guaranteed under any constitution. This demarcates the socialist state, the dictatorship of the proletariat, from the bourgeois constitutions with their formal declarations of rights.

At the same time when it is a question of provisions assuring individual liberty in relation to the state, freedom from the arbitrary behaviour on the part of the administration and the state we find a big gap. There are no checks and counter-checks against abuse of authority, and for the proper implementation of decisions, as there are in consonance with the party and the Soviets.

Comparing the provisions of the 1936 (Stalin) constitution with the new (1977) constitution of the USSR it becomes clear that the framers of the present constitution have introduced new safeguards to protect individual liberties, in an attempt to remove the weaknesses of the earlier constitution.

The 1936 constitution guarantees basic rights which only a socialist constitution and dictatorship of the proletariat can guarantee. They include the right to work, right to rest and leisure, right to maintenance in old age and also in the case of sickness or disability, right to education, equal rights for women, equality of rights of citizens of the USSR irrespective of their nationality or race, freedom of conscience, freedom of religious worship and anti-religious propaganda. Such basic fundamental rights are unheard of under a regime of an oppressing class, and they give genuine content to democracy for the people. And, as the facts about the progress of the USSR show, these rights did not remain general declarations but were all enjoyed in practice. This of course is the basic feature of a socialist constitution which frees the oppressed classes from all exploitation, and guarantees them, as a class, all rights associated with freedom from exploitation.

On the freedom of the individual, the constitution declares,

> In conformity with the interests of the working people, and in order to strengthen the socialist system, the citizens of the USSR are guaranteed by law: a) freedom of speech, b) freedom of the press, c) freedom of assembly including the holding of mass meetings, d) freedom of street processions and demonstrations.

What guarantees are there that these rights will be allowed to be exercised, that they will not be violated by officials? Very little. Article 127 boldly states,

> Citizens of the USSR are guaranteed inviolability of the person. No person may be placed under arrest except by decision of the court or with the sanction of a procurator. The inviolability of the homes of the citizens and privacy of correspondence are protected by law.

The procurator has been given the right to arrest any person. It is not known whether he had to seek the sanction of the court for continued detention. Most probably not. Perhaps persons were arrested and detained indefinitely by the procurators.

And who is this procurator general? Article 113 says, 'Supreme supervisory power to ensure the strict observance of the law by all ministries and institutions subordinate to them, as well as by officials and citizens of the USSR generally invest in the procurator general'. Article 114 says, 'The procurator-general of the USSR is appointed by the Supreme Soviet for a term of seven years'. Article 115 says, 'Procurators of Republics, Territories, Regions. Autonomous Republics and

Autonomous Regions are *appointed* (emphasis ours) by the procurator general of the USSR for a term of five years'. Article 116 says, 'Area, district and city procurators are appointed by the procurators of the Union Republics, subject to the approval of the procurator general of the USSR, for a term of five years'. Article 117 adds, 'The organs of the procurator's office perform the functions independently of any local organs whatsoever, being subordinate solely to the procurator general of the USSR'.

The procurator general's office which has immense power to arrest persons is not responsible to any local elected organ – the Soviet. These organs have no say, no right to protect the citizens' liberty. The procurator general is appointed by the Supreme Soviet and is responsible to it only. His subordinates are responsible to none except to the procurator general. To leave so much power concentrated in the hands of officials who are responsible to one official only, is an open invitation to the growth of bureaucracy and arbitrariness.

It is strange that under the same constitution the judges are elected by Soviets at all stages, but the procurator general alone is elected by the Supreme Soviet. He alone appoints his officers. The mere fact that he is appointed by the Supreme Soviet cannot be a guarantee that his office, spread over the whole of the USSR, will function democratically. No wonder there was a wave of arbitrary arrests and trials. The constitution does not provide for any appeal to the courts against arbitrary arrest. The judges are declared independent, but independent of whom? It seems the procurator general's office could order indefinite detention of the people without the judges or any other authority being any the wiser.

It is difficult to understand why this enormous concentration of authority was considered necessary in a constitution when, according to Stalin, there was hardly any one to suppress at home, when the counter-revolutionary classes were suppressed, when exploitation was eliminated and at best only spies and foreign agents were to be arrested. But perhaps it was this last excuse that was responsible for this concentration. It was thought, and wrongly so, that power would be used only against traitors, and citizens had nothing to fear. This completely went against the entire earlier experience which showed that bureaucratism, favouritism etc., were in evidence. And besides it seems that the statement of Stalin about the homogenous character of Soviet society also was an exaggerated assessment. It did not leave scope for minority opinion, dissidence and difference of opinion which often came to be identified with enemy machinations.

The 1977 Constitution contains several articles which are intended to overcome the shortcomings of the Stalin constitution, its weaknesses in relation to protection of individual liberties.

In the first place the constitution guarantees all the earlier basic rights – right to work, leisure, education, equal rights for women, rights to education, etc., some new rights are added. The right to housing is newly added. Another addition is the right to enjoy cultural benefits. Article 47 lays down that 'Citizens of the USSR, in accordance with the aims of building communism, are guaranteed freedom of scientific, technical and artistic work . . . . the rights of authors, inventors and innovators are protected by the state'.

The additions of a basic right like right to housing are fully in the conformity with the developed socialism in the USSR.

How do matters stand in relation to individual liberty? Have the drafters of the constitution realised that even under developed socialism, the individual does stand in need of protection against the state machinery? Have they grasped the lesson of the earlier period? They do seem to have, because there are a number of new provisions which specially promise protection to individuals against officialdom, which provide avenues for redress when a citizen is wronged. These provisions were absent in the earlier constitution.

The constitution guarantees freedom of speech, etc., inviolability of person and honour, and privacy of the citizen's correspondence, as in the previous constitution. Article 56 includes privacy of telephonic conversation and telegraphic communication, along with legal protection for correspondence. Article 57 is a totally new addition granting the citizens the right to go to the court to seek redress against encroachment of their rights. There was no such provision in the earlier constitution. The article also enjoins on the officials the duty to protect the rights of the citizens. The article says,

> Respect for the individual and protection of the rights and freedom of citizens are the duty of all state bodies, public organizations and officials. Citizens of the USSR have the right to protection by the courts against encroachments on their honour and reputation, life and health, and personal freedom and property.

Article 58 goes still further,

> Citizens of the USSR have the right to lodge a complaint against the actions of officials, state bodies and public bodies. Complaints shall be examined according to the procedure and within the time limits established, by law. Actions by officials that contravene the law or exceed their powers, and infringe on the right of citizens, may be appealed against in a court in the manner prescribed by law. Citizens of the USSR have the right to compensation for damage resulting from unlawful actions by State organizations, and public organizations, or by officials in the performance of their duties.

That these provisions which are to be found in bourgeois

democratic constitutions were not included in the earlier constitution, that they were included for the first time after sixty years of socialism, shows how the question of a proper relationship between the rights of the individual and the state was neglected, and took a distorted form.

Another new Article – Article 49 – says,

> Every citizen of the USSR has the right to submit proposals to state bodies and public organizations for improving their activity and to criticize shortcomings in their work. Officials are obliged, within established time limits, to examine citizens' proposals and requests, to reply to them and to take appropriate action. Persecution for criticism is prohibited. Persons guilty of such persecution shall be called to account.

That a special provision has to be made to protect criticism shows the lack of individual liberty under the previous constitution and the complete sway of officialdom over the people, the former alone being identified with the proletarian dictatorship. However, the introduction of this provision does again contribute towards extension of individual liberty and freedom and is to be welcomed. It shows that the framers of the new constitution have correctly understood the lines along which changes have to be introduced.

EXPERIENCE NOT FULLY MASTERED

But the procurator and his establishment continue to have concentrated powers as before and have the power of arresting citizens. Article 54 says, 'No one may be arrested except by a court decision or on the warrant of a procurator'. The procurator general, as in the earlier constitution, exercises supreme power of supervision over observance of law by all, including ministries, state organizations, executive administrative bodies of local Soviets of People's Deputies, collective farms, officials and citizens, etc. The procurator general is appointed by the Supreme Soviet. After his appointment the elective principle ceases to obtain. All judges at various levels are elected by the competent body of the Soviets. But the procurator general of the USSR, having been appointed by the Supreme Soviet for five years, in turn appoints procurators of Union Republics, Autonomous Republics, Territories Regions and Autonomous Regions. The agencies of the procurators' office exercise their powers independently of any local bodies whatsoever, and are subordinate solely to the procurator general of the USSR. The old articles have not been changed at all. They have been exactly reproduced in the new constitution. Here there seems to be no learning from experience.

The 1936 constitution as well as the present constitution contains articles guaranteeing freedom of speech, freedom of press, freedom of assembly, couched in almost identical terms, which perhaps indicates that the experience of the past is not fully mastered.

Article 50 of the 1977 constitution says,

> In accordance with the interests of the people, and in order to strengthen and develop the socialist system, citizens of the USSR are guaranteed freedom of speech, of the press and of assembly, meetings, street processions and demonstrations. Exercise of these political freedoms is ensured by putting public buildings, streets and squares at the disposal of the working people and their organizations, by broad dissemination of information, and by the opportunity to use the press, television and radio.

In almost identical terms the 1936 constitution also guaranteed these freedoms and yet every one realises that there were violations and the promised freedoms were not in full operation.

The identical form of declaration shows that the real weaknesses are not spotted. The declaration is still in terms of the freedom of the oppressed class which was a historic step forward taken by the successful revolution. At that time it was very correct to state that the freedoms promised to the oppressed class were not illusory, they were made real by placing at the disposal of the liberated class the wherewithal like public buildings and freedom of the street. The present constitution parrot-like repeats the former refrain.

Is 'Exercise of these political freedoms ensured by putting public buildings, streets and squares at the disposal of the working people, etc.' enough after the experience of years of socialism under the previous constitution? The point is that the material means for ensuring these rights are in the hands of the proletarian state. This is a historic advance; but the question is how the individual members of the class are assured of the exercise of this right. The main question relates to minority opinions, to people who differ from the ruling policies; the question is how far the freedom of such people to protest against what they consider to be wrong policies – protest within the framework of socialism – how far their criticism of officials, party leaders, legislators, financial measures of the government, etc., are allowed to be expressed. Here is the specific question of ensuring exercise of freedom of opinion, freedom of the press, etc., arising in connection with those who hold a differing view than the current view. It should be realised that this question is not answered by the general statement that the material means of exercising this right are no longer in the hands of an oppressing class, that they are controlled by the liberated class. Experience has shown that despite the assurance of these rights, there has been an enormous growth of bureaucracy and discouragement and stifling of legitimate criticism. Unless special provisions and guarantees are offered to encourage legitimate expression of differences, unless such people are provided with the means to express them through the press, the guaranteed freedoms will mean freedom for conformism.

It is absolutely essential for the expansion of democracy under the dictatorship of the proletariat, that public opinion feels free to express itself within the framework of socialism for or against the policies pursued, and further feels that it has a hand in shaping policies for the development of socialism. The people should not feel that they are mere objects of the policies of the party but also its subjects. This has been the weakness of the functioning of the proletarian democracy in relation to the role of the individual in the collective.

27TH CONGRESS DECISIONS

But it seems that much had not changed during the last ten years. This is clear from the recent speeches of Comrade Gorbachev. It is now realised that there should be changes in the electoral laws so that the elections represent full expression of popular will. It is also realised that the openness or freedom of expression should be legalized and given legal protection. 'Eventually the time has come to begin legal acts guaranteeing openness. These should ensure maximum openness in the activities of the state and public organizations and give the working people a real opportunity to express their opinion on any aspect of society' (Gorbachev, Speech to the Plenary Meeting of the Central Committee of the CPSU, 27-28 January 1987).

Why this was not done during the last ten years through the 1977 constitution is not known. But the reason is obvious. After ten years of the 1977 constitution, a law for bringing to book the erring bureaucrats is still to be drafted. 'We must very strictly observe the democratic principles of justice, the equality of citizens before the law, and other guarantees that protect the interest of the state and every citizen. In this context it is necessary to take vigorous steps . . . and to complete in the very near future the drafting of the law, as provided by the constitution, on the procedure of filing appeals to courts against any unlawful activity by officials that infringes the rights of the citizens' (*Report to the 27th Congress*).

All this should show that during the last two decades there has been a growing recognition of the weak points in the functions of the proletarian state. It is now being realised that notwithstanding the establishment of a new society, rid of class domination, the problem of a proper relationship between the state and the individual remains. At the same time it has to be stated that the existing awareness is not sufficiently sharp to meet the problem and solve it. The guarantees for individual freedom and freedom of expression are being worked out extremely slowly, and even the provisions made in the constitution are not in reality implemented. The decisions of the 27th Congress have raised expectations that along with accelerated economic development there will be acceleration in the understanding of the problem that has been dogging the proletarian state since its inception.

The individual freedom required in the proletarian state has nothing in common with permissiveness or freedom from duty towards the state and society, or freedom to undermine the framework of socialism. It is freedom which contributes to all round strengthening of the socialist society by the free exercise of popular expression. The enemies of socialism understand by freedom, the freedom to undermine the socialist society. This, of course, has to be fought; but all earlier restrictions following from the intensiveness of class struggle and the unfavourable correlation of contending class forces, which are now no longer necessary, must go. This is what is being done in the economic sphere. This is what is being attempted also in the political sphere after the 27th Congress. The clean sweep on such out-dated restrictions is necessary to realise the objective of economic development, corresponding to the present stage of the technological revolution and the further progress of an established and advanced socialist society.

While recognizing these weaknesses in the functioning of the proletarian state, all must combat the pernicious propaganda of imperialism about violation of human rights under socialism and presenting the socialist state as a totalitarian dictatorship. It is also to be remembered that notwithstanding some of these weaknesses, it is only in the proletarian state that people are free from class exploitation, economic miseries and class domination.

The 27th Congress decisions also propose to strengthen the collective participation of the people in all social activities, their supremacy in other activities of society. The trade unions, the collective farms, the cooperatives, the Young Communist League, the factory committees, all are to be made responsible for their involvement in economic and democratic functioning of the state and society. This is something totally different to what is possible in bourgeois societies. Coupled with the new proposals to facilitate expression of the popular will, including the freedom to criticize from below, these measures if properly pursued, will, no doubt, bring about a radical change in the democratic functioning of the state. The specificity of these measures is that they are not content with giving the right of vote to the people, the right of criticism; but they make it possible for the people to express their will and participate in other spheres of social activities, political, economic, cultural, legal etc. asserting the supremacy and sovereignty of the people. In the bourgeois state, the people of the working class have no constructive role to play in the activities of the society; they have to do their masters' bidding. Under socialism everything is open to the working class.

Notwithstanding certain weaknesses observed under the

proletarian state, the dictatorship of the proletariat has played a great historical and transitory role opening the door to a new civilization. This is the great triumph of Marxism-Leninism.

KEY ROLE OF THE PARTY

The problem of the relationship between the proletarian state and the individual cannot be considered in isolation from the key role of the Marxist-Leninist party. In a successful proletarian revolution, the building of socialism and the dictatorship of the proletariat, the role of the Marxist-Leninist party as the vanguard of the working class plays a key role. The party is the instrument of the class dictatorship; its guiding role is therefore vital. Almost everything depends on the maturity of the party; the correctness of its assessment, the devotion of its individuals, the quality of its members and their consciousness. If the party leadership, its members or the organization lose their contact with the people, get affected either by complacency, bureaucratism, overestimation of their strength, and rely on administrative measures when persuasion and change of consciousness is necessary, then calamitous results will follow. And the communist party, as the ruling party, requires a constant check exercised by the class and the masses, and by its own self-criticism.

The vigilance of the masses as the corrective to the party's shortcomings, was recommended by Lenin. 'In some places', he wrote, 'the purging of the party is proceeding mainly with the aid of the experience and suggestions of non-party workers; these suggestions are being heeded, and the representatives of the non-party proletarian masses are being treated with due consideration. This is most valuable and most important. If we really succeed *in this manner* in purging our party from top to bottom, *without respect for persons* the gains for the revolution will really be enormous.'

Both Lenin and Stalin understood the necessity of constant correction of the party and its weaknesses by the masses. Both understood it as vitally necessary in conditions of the dictatorship of the proletariat, when the party functions as the instrument of class dictatorship. If the party goes wrong on any count, especially if it does not constantly listen to the voice of the masses, mistakes are bound to occur. And they did occur under Stalin because, in practice, the free criticism of the masses as well members, was not encouraged and welcomed, and the growth of bureaucratism demanded its restriction more and more. Such a development divorces the party from its class, and distorts its role of vanguard and guidance.

Lenin had clearly distinguished between the dictatorship of the party and the dictatorship of the working class. He put this idea in the following words,

> On the whole we have a formally non-communist, flexible and relatively powerful proletarian apparatus [Lenin means the mass organizations like the trade unions, cooperatives, Soviets – Ranadive] by means of which the party is closely linked with the class and with the masses, and by means of which under the leadership of the party, the dictatorship of the class is exercised.

The ruling proletarian party, in so far as it isolates itself from the mass on any particular aspect of social life and rides roughshod over them, to that extent substitutes the dictatorship of the party for the dictatorship of the proletariat.

Despite this understanding that the constant correction by the masses was required, bureaucratism did invade the party apparatus, and following it, the state apparatus. Why? Because individualism and bureaucratism are the toughest survivals of capitalist habits, of bourgeois-feudal habits, that require a constant battle for years to eradicate them, and to hold them in check; constant vigilance and special provisions to combat them are necessary. The party is the most vital instrument in this struggle, but the party members themselves are not free from this habit and hence the vital character of this struggle.

Lenin, and the Bolshevik party saw the danger of this deviation, warned the party against it, and took steps from time to time to overcome it. The fact that they often failed, shows the tough character of the struggle.

What steps did Lenin suggest? In 1923 Lenin wrote,

> Our Central Committee has grown into a strictly centralized and highly authoritative group, but the conditions under which this group is working are not commensurate with its authority. The reform I recommend should help to remove this defect, and the members of the Control Commission, whose duty it will be to attend all meetings of the Political Bureau in a definite number, will have to form a compact group which should not allow anybody's authority, without exception, neither that of the General Secretary nor of any other member of the Central Committee, to prevent them from putting questions, verifying documents, and in general, from keeping themselves fully informed of all things and from exercising the strictest control over the proper conduct of affairs.[14]

Stalin addressing the 17th Congress of the CPSU(B) in 1934 said,

> But on the other hand, there is an imperative need for an organization that could concentrate its attention mainly on checking up on the fulfilment of the decisions of the party and of its central committee. Such an organization can be only a

[14] *Collected Works*, Vol. 33, p. 485.

party Control Commission under the Central Committee of the CPSU(B), working on the assignments of the party and its Central Committee and having local representatives who are independent of the local organizations. It goes without saying that such a responsible organization must have great authority. In order that it may have sufficient authority and in order that it may be able to take proceedings against any delinquent comrade holding a responsible post, including members of the Central Committee, the right to elect or dismiss the members of the Commission must be vested only in the supreme organ of the party, viz., the party congress. There can be no doubt that such an organization will be quite capable of ensuring control over the fulfilment of the decisions of the central organs of the party and of tightening up party discipline.[15]

And again,

But testing from above far from exhausts the whole business of checking up. There is still another kind of check up, the check-up from below, where the masses, the subordinates, examine the leaders, point out their mistakes, and show them ways of correcting them. This kind of verification is one of the most effective methods of testing people.

The rank and file party members verify their leaders at meetings of active party workers, and conferences and congresses, by listening to their reports, by criticizing their defects, and finally by electing or not electing some or other leading comrades to leading party organs. Precise operation of democratic centralism in the party as demanded in our party statutes, unconditional submission of party organs to election, the right of putting forward and withdrawing candidates, secret ballot, freedom of criticism and self-criticism, all these and

[15] *Problems of Leninism*, p. 651.

> similar measures must be carried into life in order incidentally to facilitate the check up and control over the leaders of the party by the rank and file of the party members.
>
> The non-party masses verify their economic, trade union and other leaders in meetings of non-party workers, at all kinds of mass conferences, when they hear reports of their leaders, criticize defects and indicate ways of correcting them.[16]

Here there is realisation of how to avoid bureaucracy in the party and how to keep this vital instrument of the dictatorship of the proletariat free from any taint of bureaucratic behaviour. But as subsequent events have shown, this understanding did not help the CPSU(B), and bureaucratism accompanied by the personality cult developed in the party, leading to dangerous consequences. It only showed that the battle against bureaucratism is one of the toughest in the fight against survivals of capitalism in the minds of the people.

Two conclusions follow. Firmer guarantees for individual liberties must be embodied in the constitution and the party must devote far greater attention to safeguard its own purity, knowing that the struggle against the growth of bureaucratic tendencies is among the toughest.

It is clear that Stalin contributed to this development, despite his clear understanding of the problem, through some of his personal shortcomings. He concentrated too much power in his hands – power which came to him through his outstanding abilities, and set a pattern of functioning which led to individualism and the cult of personality.

Lenin had already sized up some of his dangerous weaknesses.

> Comrade Stalin, having become Secretary-General, has

[16] *Selected Writings*, Vol. II, pp. 73-74.

> unlimited authority concentrated in his hands, and I am not sure whether he will always be capable of using that authority with sufficient caution . . . Stalin is too rude and this defect, although quite tolerable in our midst and in dealings among us communists, becomes intolerable in a Secretary-General. That is why I suggest that the comrades think about a way of removing Stalin from the post and appointing another man in his stead who, in all other respects, differs from Comrade Stalin in having only one advantage, namely, that of being more tolerant, more loyal, more polite and more considerate to the comrades, less capricious, etc.[17]

The question of the free expression of popular will is not restricted to the relationship between the individual and the state. Under the proletarian state it is related also to the relationship between the non-party masses and the Marxist-Leninist party, the guiding force of the society and the state. It is also related to inner party democracy. The cult of personality under Stalin and Mao led to the erosion of inner party democracy, and also complicated the relationship between the party and the masses. Communist parties in many socialist countries have criticized themselves for violation of inner party democracy. Partly perhaps, this was due to the fact that the ways and methods of the earlier period when the proletarian party was conducting a revolutionary fight and had to remain underground, remained unchanged after the conquest of power. The party is a vital instrument in the functioning of the proletarian state. Democracy, freedom of individuals and of criticism under the proletarian state, must include freedom to express not only opinion about the party line and party's policies. It must also ensure freedom of expression for party members inside the party. Otherwise

[17] *Collected Works*, Vol. 36, p. 596.

the judgements and the decisions of the party will cease to be expressive of the collective will and are likely to be wrong on many occasions.

Again it is seen that after the exposures of undermining of inner party democracy under Stalin the proper lessons were not drawn. The same earlier ideas about the party continue and criticism and self-criticism are not properly applied, and even sometimes are punished. This is clear from Gorbachev's speech to the Plenary meeting of the CPSU Central Committee,

> The school of re-organization does not come easy to some party leaders. They cannot yet give up the dispatcher functions so unnatural for party committees, the wish to decide all questions for everyone and keep a tight grip on things. But this, as always, hampers growth in the responsibility of the cadres for the work they have been entrusted with, the development of their initiative and independence.
>
> Instead of developing innovative thinking, the party officials quite often react adversely to the initiative and activeness of people and view them as almost a natural calamity. But the paramount duty of the party committees in the conditions of reorganization is to guide the creativity of the masses, help people eliminate shortcomings, and get down to work as soon as possible.

This criticism would not have been necessary had there been a growing awareness of the weaknesses in the relationship between the party and the masses, and the relationship between the leadership and the members, during the last three decades. It will be seen that changes have been introduced without changing the earlier concept about the party functioning. The 27th Congress of the CPSU has also now introduced new rules for greater democratic functioning of the party, for inner-party democracy, and at the same time it has also called for greater freedom of discussion and greater openness in society. All these put together are expected to change the old situation and remove all distortions for the functioning of the party. There is no doubt that this awareness and the new rules are welcome, and they will definitely tend to help create a greater sense of responsibility and freedom among the people. But it would be wrong to expect that they will bring about a qualitative change unless the basic defect in the relationship between the party and the masses is removed.

RELATIONSHIP BETWEEN THE PARTY & THE STATE

The problem is complicated because of the overwhelming role of the communist party under the dictatorship of the proletariat. Marxism-Leninism correctly asserts that the party is the instrument of the dictatorship of the proletariat. The party is the vanguard of the working class and without its guiding role the affairs of the proletarian state cannot be conducted, its tactics relating to allies, its firm suppression of the class enemies and building of socialism – all of which demand firm commitment and knowledge of Marxist-Leninist theory, which only the party possesses. The party, starting as a revolutionary organization of proletarian revolution, historically develops into a lynch-pin of the proletarian socialist state. Stalin in his speech on the 1936 constitution proudly proclaimed that it openly declares the leading role of the party. 'I must admit that the draft of the new constitution does preserve the regime of the dictatorship of the working class, first as it also preserves unchanged the present leading positions of the Communist Party of the USSR. If the esteemed critics regard this as a flaw in the Draft Constitution, that is only to be regretted. We Bolsheviks regard it as a merit of the Draft Constitution' (*Problems of Leninism, p.* 557).

The 1936 Constitution puts the role of the party in the following words.

> In conformity with the interests of the working people, and in order to develop organizational initiative and political activity of the masses of the people, citizens of the USSR are guaranteed the right to unite in public organizations, trade unions, cooperative societies, youth organizations, sport and defence organizations, cultural, technical, and scientific societies; and the most *active and politically conscious citizens in the ranks of the working class and other sections of the working people unite in the Communist Party of the Soviet Union (Bolsheviks), which is the vanguard of the working people in their struggle to strengthen and develop the socialist system and is the leading core of all organizations of the working people, both public and state* (Article 126).

The 1977 constitution states the same role of the party in Article 6 which says,

> The leading and guiding force of Soviet society and the nucleus of its political system, of all state organizations and public organizations, is the Communist Party of the Soviet Union. The CPSU exists for the people and serves the people.
>
> The Communist Party, armed with Marxism-Leninism, determines the general perspective of the development of society and the course of the home and foreign policy of the USSR, directs the great constructive work of the Soviet people and imparts a planned, systematic and theoretically substantiated character to their struggle for the victory of communism.
>
> All party organizations shall function within the framework of the constitution of the USSR.

One may ask what is left for the state machinery, if the party is to determine all these matters. Firstly, the question is, should the vanguard role of the party become a principle or article of the constitution? Is it a constitutional, juridical and legal concept? And by constitutionalizing the leading role of the party in this way, does not the supremacy of the constitution get denigrated; does not the dictatorship of the proletariat, not to be confused with the dictatorship of the party, get denigrated? Does it not tend to reduce the dictatorship of the class to the dictatorship of the party?

It is true that the communist party which has organized the revolution and without whose guiding role the dictatorship of the proletariat cannot function and socialism be built should find a place in the constitution. Would it not have been enough to state the bald truth that the communist party is the instrument of realising the dictatorship of the proletariat, which statement properly defines the relationship between the party and the proletarian state?

Should the guiding role of the party be put in a manner which seems to provide all power to the party and render superfluous the state bodies so far as policy decisions are concerned. If the communist party determines the perspective of the development of society, determines the course of home and foreign policy, and directs the great constructive work of the Soviet people, what remains for the Supreme Soviet and the elected Soviet bodies. The constitution itself lays down that the vital policies will be determined by the party. This is substitution of a part of the class for the whole class. This is a distortion of the guiding and leading role of the party which is ensured through constant and correct guidance of the class, and its acceptance by the latter, and not constitutionally imposed. A way has to be found to express correctly the role of the party as the instrument of proletarian rule, without giving the impression that it stands above the state of the class and its bodies.

LEADING ROLE OF THE PARTY AND RIGHT TO CRITICISM

The incorporation of the leading role of the party in the constitution itself puts extremely heavy responsibilities on the party. If they are not realised and steps are not taken to meet them, old mistakes are likely to be repeated. It is obvious that the present leadership of the CPSU is keen on avoiding the old mistakes. But it may not be possible to avoid them unless the present provisions in the constitution and the claim to expand citizens' liberties are fulfilled.

We have already discussed how the preponderingly large powers of the procurator general militate against safeguarding and ensuring of individual liberties. The new openings offered in the constitution though extremely well-intentioned, are too weak to ensure them beyond doubt. The same situation exists in relation to the party. Having proclaimed a preponderant role to the party in the constitution, having declared it a vanguard which determines policies, it is incumbent on the party to tell the people that they have a right to criticize the party, its mistakes, and that it is their democratic duty to correct its mistakes. In the absence of such an assurance who would dare criticize the party or point out its errors? In terms of the constitutions, it may appear seditious to criticize an organization constitutionally certified as the vanguard; it may be interpreted as refusal to accept the vanguard role of the party, and stifle all criticism as happened in the past.

It is noteworthy that this is precisely what is lacking in the 1977 constitution.

> Every citizen of the USSR has the right to submit proposals to State bodies and public organizations for improving their activity and to criticize shortcomings in their work. Officials are obliged, within established time-limits, to examine citizens' proposals and requests, to reply to them, to take appropriate action. Persecution for criticism is prohibited. Persons guilty of such persecution shall be called to account (Article 49).

The party is nowhere mentioned. Can you submit proposals to the party and criticize its shortcomings? Are you in that case granted protection against persecution? It seems no. You may criticize officials, public bodies, etc., but the party is not mentioned. This is bound to lead to distortions. The people should be free to express to the party their opinion on vital issues – not just on select issues presented by the party to them. The party should be in a position to gather public opinion and criticism to be on correct lines and, above all, avoid the prevalence of bureaucratism in its ranks. Lack of such exchange of views hardens the bureaucratic tendency in the party and leads to a paternal and patronizing attitude towards the masses.

THE GORBACHEVIAN REFORMS: DISMANTLING THE COMMUNIST PARTY (1991)

Prakash Karat

Mikhail Gorbachev, former General Secretary of the CPSU, spent 7 November 1991, the 74th anniversary of the October revolution, alone in the Kremlin. He did not participate in the traditional parade at the Red Square, for there was no parade; he did not attend any Party celebrations, for the Party did not exist having been banned and made illegal. All he did was attend a meeting at the Kremlin to give away State awards – one of the remnants of the power vested with Union Government whose scope and jurisdiction was fast shrinking.

Six years earlier, Mikhail Gorbachev was elected the General Secretary of the Central Committee of the CPSU, after the death of Konstantin Chernenko. In April 1985 at the Central Committee plenary meeting he initiated his plans for restructuring and acceleration of production. In February 1986 the economic and political forms mooted by him won overwhelming endorsement. But in five years time, the Gorbachev reforms ended in disaster both for socialism and the unity of the Soviet Union. The CPSU stood dismantled.

SIX YEARS OF DISASTROUS TRANSFORMATION

The unfolding of the Gorbachevian reforms of *perestroika* (restructuring) and *glasnost* (openness) eventually led to the process of restoration of capitalism and the disintegration of the Soviet Union. A key to understanding why such a cataclysmic transformation took place lies in the role of the CPSU. Between the 27th Party Congress in February 1986 and the July 1991 Central Committee Plenum the Gorbachevian reforms had a drastic and shattering effect on the Party. The

CPSU from being the initiator and vanguard in ushering in reforms for socialist renewal soon became a party in disarray – ideologically, politically and organizationally. It is vital to understand how this disastrous transformation came about under the leadership of Gorbachev and his trusted colleagues. How is it that the Party founded by Lenin which had faced many challenges and crisis situations could become a vehicle for the disintegration of the Soviet Union and the socialist system? The answer to this provides important insights into the downfall of the CPSU and the debacle for socialism in the Soviet Union.

The main focus of this article is on the six years of perestroika. It does not cover the historical period of the post-1917 decades. No doubt, the period preceding the advent of Gorbachev to the leadership of the CPSU has an important bearing on the internal crisis within the party and the inner-party struggles. The six-year period is taken up as it provides object lessons for Communists on what should be avoided and combatted if the Communist Party is to play its leading role in building and advancing socialism.

What was the new orientation which led the CPSU into an ideological dead-end? What were the political positions which enabled the anti-socialist forces to gain the commanding positions in Soviet society? And finally what were the organizational principles advocated and practised which destroyed party unity and left the multi-million Communist Party members disarmed and in total disarray?

The political and ideological positions evolved by the CPSU is not being dealt with in detail here. The focus is on the effects of these positions on the Party and its organizational manifestations.

The dismantling of the CPSU after the August events is an unprecedented phenomenon. Never before in history has a party which led an authentic socialist revolution surrendered so abjectly before the onslaught of the forces of counter-revolution.

As General Secretary of the Central Committee of the Party, there are three phases in Gorbachev's dealing with the Party. In the first phase between 1985-86, Gorbachev exuded confidence in the Party being able to remould itself and face up to the new challenges. In the second phase, from 1987 to 1988, he continued to emphasize the Party role as initiator and considered only some elements incapable of changing to the new outlook and methods. Upto this period, the exhortations to the Party to be the vanguard of perestroika is couched in an appeal to return to Leninist traditions. But by 1987, the inner-struggle sharpened and he begins warning that those who do not change will fall by the wayside. In the last phase, the tone becomes strident, the Party is seen to be lagging behind the momentum of perestroika, acting as an obstacle in many ways. This period , from 1989 to 1990, sets the backdrop for the rapid disorganization of the Party and the theoretical and practical steps which disarm the Party.

APPEAL IN THE LENINIST MOULD

At the 27th Congress, in his political report, Gorbachev noted with pride,

> The Party's strength is that it has a feel for the time . . . whenever the country faces new problems the Party finds ways of resolving them, restructures and remoulds leadership methods, demonstrating its ability to measure up to its historic responsibility for the country's destiny, for the cause of socialism and communism.

Gorbachev's plans for economic restructuring and political reforms in the early period stressed the Party's central role in ushering in change and socialist renewal. He stated that the Party must be the engine of perestroika. There is the constant theme of a return to Leninist methods of organization. Gorbachev's thrust seemed to be to reorganize the Party so that it could be able to play its leading role in the restructuring process. In the Central Committee Plenum held in January 1987 a major report was presented by Gorbachev on the 'Reorganization and the Party's personnel policy'. In the concluding speech at this Plenum he said,

> At the Plenary meeting today we have repeatedly referred to Lenin, his thoughts and ideas .... This reflects the pressing desire to revive in modern conditions and to the fullest possible extent the spirit of Leninism, to assert in our life the Leninist demands on personnel. You will recall, Comrades, how passionately how tirelessly Lenin taught us that the success of the revolutionary struggle, the success of any cardinal restructuring of society is largely determined by the tone set by the Party.

In the early period it appeared that Gorbachev was goading the Party leadership to realise the seriousness of the situation, overcome their inertia and take the responsibility for leading the reform process. He was sharply critical of the responsibility of the Party for the stagnation and negative tendencies in society. In the January 1987 report it was stated,

> The main cause – and the Political Bureau considers it necessary to say so with utmost frankness at the Plenary Meeting – was that the CPSU Central Committee and the leadership of the country failed, primarily for subjective reasons, to see in time and in full the need for change and the dangerous growth of crisis phenomena in society, and to formulate a clear-cut policy for overcoming them and making better use of the possibilities intrinsic to the socialist system.

Continuing in this vein the report directly pinpointed the responsibility of the Party,

> The state of the Party and its personnel also affected the socio-economic and political situation that took shape in the late 1970s and early 1980s. Leading Party bodies failed to timely and critically appraise the danger of the growing negative tendencies in society and in the conduct of some Communists, and to take decisions which life was imperatively demanding.

Assessing the changed outlook of the Party as a whole Gorbachev was optimistic about the Party's capacity to reorient itself to accelerate change. He said,

> Today we can say that most Party committees and their leaders have got down to work with a great sense of responsibility and a sincere desire. They are not yet able to cope with many things, but they are gaining experience and confidence with every passing day. These changes create reliable prerequisites for accelerating our advance.

However, in this Central Committee meeting he gave the first warning to those who would not be able to change, 'All the Party workers are going through the test of reorganization. But they stand it differently. Reorganization does not come easy to some Party leaders'.

The period 1985-87 saw the ascendancy of Gorbachev's leadership in the Party organization in terms of large-scale replacement of leading Party functionaries at various levels. At the April 1985 Central Committee Plenum Gorbachev received a mandate for restructuring and consolidation of the line. The period saw rapid changes in the Party leadership at all levels. In the 27th Congress more than 50 per cent of the full Central Committee members were retired, the highest percentage of change since the 1961 Congress when Khrushchev was the General Secretary.

The changes at the lower Party Committees were more drastic which astounded those who closely observed Soviet Party affairs. The chart below indicates the scale of the change,

Replacement/removal of leading Party cadres
March 1985 to August 1987

First Secretaries of Republic Party Committees
6 out of 14
First Secretaries, Party oblast Committees
75 out of 150
Voting members of republic Party Bureaus
84 out of 163
All Secretaries of Party oblast Committees
almost 50 percent
Secretaries of city and district Committees
almost 50 percent

At no time in the history of the CPSU, except in the early period under Stalin's leadership, were so many changes made in the leadership at all levels. It may be necessary at different stages in a Party's history to radically change the Party's leading personnel to cope with the new tasks by rejuvenating the Party organization. The question is what is the shake-up for? It soon became evident that the 'restructuring of Party personnel' was not for overcoming bureaucratic inertia. Gorbachev was bent upon purging the Party to overcome resistance to bourgeois reforms and social democracy.

With all these changes the Gorbachevian leadership would have expected a smooth course in implementing their policy measures. Yet, there is evidence that Gorbachev met with persistent resistance in the Central Committee. That is why by mid-1987 he began airing the need for convening an All-Union Conference. At the June 1987 Central Committee Plenum he suddenly suggested the holding of the All-Union Party Conference, the last of which had been held 46 years ago. Intense reporting and election campaigning was to precede the holding of the Conference. Underlying the convening of the Conference was the threat to the Central Committee that the Conference would be used to elect new members of the Central Committee. The election of delegates to the Conference did not eliminate 'the conservative opposition' as much as Gorbachev hoped it would. In fact the liberals publicly raised a hue and cry about the elimination of their supporters in the election process. Gorbachev himself later stated that the leadership had considered making a provision for changes in the Central Committee but had given up the idea. This, in hindsight, he thought was expedient. But the drive to eliminate the Party opposition was continued in new forms after the All-Union Conference.

THE TURNING POINT: THE 19TH ALL-UNION CONFERENCE

The convening of the 19th All-Union Conference of the CPSU in June 1988 was a turning point in the internal affairs of the Party. Prior to this, Gorbachev, for all the talk of restructuring and reforms, had been unable to show results. The year 1987 showed a deterioration in the economic situation. The tone of the Gorbachevian leadership changed. Instead of exhortations to the Party, critical remarks that the Party leaders at different levels were unable to change and adapt to perestroika and glasnost began to be voiced. From this followed the conclusion that there must be drastic overhauling of the Party organization and the Central apparatus. At the All-Union Conference the report took up the critical refrain on the Party. The General Secretary posed the question, 'why we subject the state of affairs in our Party home to bitter criticism. What is the matter?' He proceeds to give the answer, 'The matter is, in the first place, that the principle of democratic centralism, which underlies the structure and activity of the CPSU, was at a certain stage largely replaced by bureaucratic centralism.' From this point onwards a determined effort was made to scrap democratic centralism itself in the name of eliminating bureaucratic centralism and command-administer methods. This struggle continued up to the 28th Congress and was not resolved till the time of the July 1991 Central Committee meeting which decided to convene the 29th Congress of the Party. At the 19th All-Union Conference and the 28th Congress of the CPSU, the efforts to dilute democratic centralism or bypass it were resisted by the majority of the Central Committee and the delegates.

One of the principles correctly enunciated in the report was the demarcation of the functions of the Party and the state bodies. Gorbachev cited Lenin, 'Lenin repeatedly pointed out to the harmful nature of the notion that a governing party must directly administer, ignoring or replacing other organizations of the working people'.

But the report goes on to recommend an astonishing proposal which runs completely counter to the principle of demarcation. It proposes combining the post of General Secretary of the CPSU and the newly created President's post to be elected by the Congress of Deputies. After expounding on the virtues of this enormous concentration of powers by combining the two posts as necessary at the critical juncture, Gorbachev proposed that this principle of combination be applied to all levels in the Party. The report states, 'Here the most practical way would be to nominate as a rule, the first Secretaries of Party committees to serve as chairman of the respective Soviets'. Such a merging of party and Soviet functions comes after the report explains elaborately the necessity for revitalizing the society, holding elections with multi-party candidates and ensuring that the elected Deputies fully participate in decision making and implementation.

But despite the obvious contradiction in the proposal, the resolution adopted at the Conference 'On democratizing Soviet society and reforming the political system' states, 'The role of the representative bodies would be enhanced if the first secretaries of respective Party Committees were, as a rule recommended to serve as the Soviet's chairperson.'

Why this flagrant violation of the principles sought to be adhered to? It was the most puzzling outcome of the 19th Conference. With hindsight now the situation can be reconstructed.

After combining the posts of General Secretary and the Presidency, Gorbachev found it expedient to apply the same principle at the lower levels. But in a manoeuvre of brilliance that became his hallmark, he proposed a 'formula' for the other Party secretaries that had factional motives.

First the unexceptionable proposal was made that the Party Secretary should be elected at a Plenary Meeting from two or more candidates by secret ballot. This measure was to strengthen inner-party democracy and allow Party delegates to exercise their right of evaluation and choice.

But then the Party secretary would have to undergo another test. The person must contest the elections to the Soviets as a Deputy. If he or she is elected then he or she must undergo another test. He or she must offer themselves for the post of the chairperson of the Soviet which is elected by the Deputies.

The reason transparently insincere, given being 'Placed at the head of the Soviets and their presidiums, they will be very active in helping improve all aspects of the work performed by the popular representative bodies.'

As for subjecting the Party secretaries to the electoral test of the Soviets, Gorbachev explained and let the cat out of the bag,

> This means that the mandate received by a Party leader from Communists will be verified and confirmed by representatives of the people each time, at all levels of the system of the Soviets. Naturally, the nomination of a Party Secretary may not always be supported by the deputies. If that is the case, the Party Committee and the Communists will obviously have to draw the necessary conclusions.

The inevitable conclusion being that he or she is unfit to be the secretary.

This whole proposal adopted at the Conference displayed Gorbachev's skill in manipulation to strengthen his position. While all first secretaries at all levels had to face the electoral test to remain in office, Gorbachev did not face an election. He was nominated to the Congress of Deputies from the CPSU quota of 100 members. In the elections which took place to the Soviets at all levels, 38 regional Party Secretaries failed to get elected. They all had to step down. It is not clear how many more had to go for their failure to be elected as chairpersons to the Soviets. Thus at one stroke Gorbachev, the initiator of perestroika, concentrated further powers in his hands while at the same time was able to get rid of a large number of Party secretaries who were elected by the Party.

This duplicity indicated the growing intensity of struggle within the Party and the factional manoeuvres, which began in this conference, became one of the main features of Party life in the forthcoming years.

Gorbachev's tactics became clear after the 19th Conference. He planned to bypass the Party now instead of 'renewing' it. In his peculiar interpretation of the Leninist principle of demarcating State and Party functions, he took steps to ensure that the Party be deprived of actual power. At the Centre after assuming the Presidentship, he created a Presidential Council. A number of Presidential decrees were passed in the sphere of the economy, the republics and on political issues. When the Party resisted being sidelined, he declared war on the Party and began a series of manoeuvres to weaken the leadership and finally ended up with him being the sole surviving leader, general secretary and executive head.

The basic weakness of those who opposed the derailment of the reforms and the anti-socialist content, was that they were also dependent on Gorbachev. Time and again, the revolt against these policies stopped in its tracks when the question of removing the General Secretary came up, or when he threatened to quit. Given the growing popularity of Yeltsin, the Party opposition saw no hopes for an alternative rallying figure but Gorbachev. Ligachev was unable to inspire such confidence or support. It was this weakness that Gorbachev took full advantage of by balancing the right wing liberals and the defenders of socialism. He aspired to and did play a Bonapartist role for some time, this in turn destroyed the chances of the Party rectifying the aberrations and deviations.

DOWNGRADING THE WORKING CLASS

Gorbachev, in his struggle for supremacy against the 'hard-liners' and the party leadership at all levels, took another major step on the eve of the 19th Conference. He endorsed the demand appearing in the media and among the intelligentsia that the class composition of the elected delegates be altered. Gorbachev in his speech to the Meeting of Media executives and Heads of Ideological Institutes on 7 May 1988 announced the new stand,

> The CPSU Central Committee has expressed its opinion on procedures for electing delegates to the Conference. Our position is that committed stalwarts of perestroika, active communists should be chosen as delegates. *There must be no more quotas, as was the case in the past, specifying how many factory workers and farmers and how many women are to be chosen, among others.* The principle political directive is to send active supporters of perestroika to the Conference. [Emphasis added.]

The quotas referred to had ensured that apart from the party leadership at all levels, the bulk of the delegates came primarily from the working class followed by the peasantry. It had ensured the dominance of working class composition so far in all elected Congresses/Conferences of the party's authoritative bodies. We saw the result of this in the 28th Congress of the CPSU held in July 1990. Out of the total delegates only 14 per cent came from the working class as compared to 46 per cent in the 27th Congress. In the Congress of Deputies and Supreme Soviet also the representation of the working class and collective farmers came down after the elections in 1989. The category of workers and collective farmers was 44.9 per cent in the Supreme Soviet in 1984, which came down to 22.8 per cent in the Congress of People's Deputies in 1989.

There is no doubt that the diminution of the working class composition in the Parry's authoritative bodies had its own impact on Party policies.

The way Gorbachev got the quotas scrapped in the Party is typical of the *modus operandi* which surfaced again and again. First the intellectuals backing the Gorbachev line would propagate the cause in the media – direct their fire against the Party 'conservatives'. Soon after the same arguments would become the official proposals for the Party mooted by

Gorbachev. In the case of the campaign against quotas, one of the articles against it was written by Yuri Burtin in the *Izvestia* on 29 April 1988. He denigrated the role of the workers and extolled that of the intelligentsia. He asked in the article,

> Developments should take their natural course. What is horrible about not a single milking machine operator or a weaver being not sent to a Soviet, even to the Supreme Soviet . . .? Will public interest suffer if the vacant seats are taken by public spirited and popular economists, historians, social workers, authors, art directors and actors?

A month later Gorbachev advocated the abolition of quotas in a Party forum for the first time. Along with this he demanded that only 'active supporters of perestroika' be elected as delegates to the 19th Conference. So much for inner-party democracy and glasnost! Those who differed with the content and direction of perestroika had no place in the Conference in Gorbachev's new stress on democracy.

PARTY MEDIA: SUBVERSION FROM WITHIN

Another important facet of the subversion within the Party was how the Party media and journalists became vehicles for denigrating the Party and disorienting Party members and destroying the common will.

Mike Davidow, a US progressive writer who closely followed Soviet developments put it well in his talk to a meeting of Moscow communists in December 1990,

> The other example is the media. One would find it hard to believe that the flood of anti-socialist, anti-Soviet, anti-Party propaganda appearing on TV and in leading newspapers and magazines, weeklies, was supervized by the Party. Many Party leaders

> have become not only ex-Communists, but anti-Communists. And they have been permitted to take over newspapers and magazines, weeklies in 'editorial collectives', which the Party, directly, and through its members in organizations, had led. Party presses publish newspapers and weeklies which steadily attack the Party and pursue an anti-socialist policy. This is the kind of glasnost and democracy even bourgeois parties in the West, the Democratic and Republican Parties in the USA would find hard to comprehend.

If sections of the Party press and media purveyed openly anti-Communist and anti-socialist propaganda, the seeds for this lie in the glasnost of the Gorbachevian leadership. At no time in the entire period of six years did Gorbachev and his close circle call upon the Party to combat anti-socialist propaganda and defamation in an organized manner. He did of course depreciate the tendency of the open press to sensationalize some historical events or present problems. But the thrust to the Party was to adjust to this new phenomenon in the name of glasnost.

It is Party members in the huge media of the CPSU and related newspapers which spearheaded the attack of the 'conservatives' and hardliners in the name of doing away with the old methods of command-administration and 'barracks-style' socialism. After the Russian Party Conference, many Party members in papers like *TASS, Novosti* and *Literaturnaya Gazeta* openly railed against the Party and many deserted.

1989-90: WAR ON THE PARTY

Armed with the mandate of the 19th Conference, Gorbachev moved quickly to consolidate his position. Within three months of the Conference, a Central Committee Plenum was hastily opened for a day on 30 September. Andrei Gromyko and Mikhail Solomentsev, two senior Politburo members were retired from the Politburo. Along with them two candidate members also stepped down, Pyotr Demichev and Vladmir Dolgikh. Vadim Medvedev who was elected as a Secretariat member only in 1988 was promoted to full member of the Politburo. Three new candidate members were elected.

The reshuffling and purges continued unabated. On 25 April 1989 an extraordinary plenum of the Central Committee was held in which 74 full Central Committee members and 24 candidates requested to be relieved of their positions due to age and health reasons. Many of them were considered to be the old guards. They included former Politburo members Andrei Gromyko, Mikail Solomentsev, Geidar Aliyev, Nikolai Tikhonov. In addition 12 out of the 82 members of the Central Control and Auditing Commission also quit.

Interestingly, their request for retirement came in the form of an appeal signed collectively by all retiring members, which indicated that the 'request' had been coordinated by the Politburo and the Secretariat. The triumphant mood of the Gorbachevian supporters was evident. Vadim Medvedev, the new Politburo member, who briefed the press, called the voluntary retirements 'a major landmark in the history of perestroika'.

The Central Committee also decided that the future of those regional party secretaries (more than thirty) who lost the elections to the Congress of deputies would be decided by their respective party committees.

In the September 1989 Central Committee Plenary meeting, more Politburo members retired: Vladimir Scherbitsky (the last surviving Politburo member of the pre-27th Congress period apart from Gorbachev), Viktor Chebrikov (former KGB chief), Viktor Nikonov and two candidates Yury Solovyev and

Nikolai Talyzin. In their places two new Politburo members were elected: Victor Kryuchkov and Maslyukov. Boris Pugo was elected as a candidate member.

The beheading of the Party leadership continued till the 28th Congress where the very concept of the Politburo itself was re-fashioned. None of the members of the Politburo of the 27th Congress remained except for Gorbachev in the body whose size was doubled. Each one of the 23 other members was new. Of these 15 were the secretaries of the Republican Party Central Committees. Gorbachev in order to fight the 'hardliners' packed the Politburo with republican secretaries who anyway would devote no time to the affairs of the Party Centre.

Even with all these changes, Gorbachev could not command a stable majority for his line in the Politburo after September 1989. It may be recalled here that apart from Ligachev and Vorotnikov in the Politburo, there were also four others who later played an important role in the August takeover attempt. They were Kryuchkov, full member and Boris Pugo, Dmitry Yazov and Anatoly Lukanov all candidate members of the Politburo.

That is why before the 28th Congress, the Draft Platform had suggested the election of a Chairman, and his deputies by the Congress. Central Committee Plenary meetings would elect a Presidium to handle political and organizational issues between sessions of the Central Committee. This drastic restructuring would have abolished the Politburo and Secretariat and the post of General Secretary as it stood so far. This was strongly opposed in the pre-Congress discussions and the Congress deleted this proposal from the Policy statement.

The bitter struggle to eliminate the 'hardliners' continued into the 28th Party Congress. This resulted in a brand new Politburo with only Gorbachev from the old Politburo! For the newly created post of Deputy General Secretary, the

Politburo's choice Ivashko defeated Ligachev by a big margin. Boris Pugo, the future 'conspirator' was elected the Chairman of the newly created Central Control Commission.

Gorbachev and his supporters used another parallel track to isolate Party resistance and to disarm it. From the turning point of the 19th Conference, Gorbachev went on to be elected as President of the Union on the basis of his nomination to the Congress of Peoples Deputies (CPD) on the CPSU quota. The Congress and Supreme Soviet voted to give sweeping executive powers to the Presidency. He created the Presidential Council which was in future to play the role of a Supreme governmental council and take away the powers of the Politburo in the sphere of Government. Those who were appointed ministers of government were obliged to leave the Politburo. Thus Ryzhkov as Prime Minister, Pugo as Interior Minister and Yazov as Defence Minister had to quit the Politburo. Lukyanov was elected Chairman of the Supreme Soviet so he also left the Politburo.

This process led to the downgrading of the Politburo on the one hand and on the other hand the concentration of powers in the hands of the President who was also the General Secretary. Ligachev, who continued in the Politburo looking after agriculture, had no post in government or the Presidential Council. He complained in June 1990 in a speech before the Constituent Congress of the Russian Communist Party 'that the CPSU leadership had begun to lose its collective spirit and democratism and stopped taking into account the opinion of others'. TASS reported Ligachev's speech,

> Ligachev expressed concern over the fact that many crucial problems are now discussed neither at the Politburo nor at Plenary Meetings of the Party Central Committee. He cited as an example the government's measures for the transition to a market economy, the analysis of the developments in Eastern

> Europe and the German Issue. The Socialist community has disintegrated, while the positions of imperialism have been dramatically consolidated.

Ligachev went on to make a significant remark whose import was not fully understood within his own party, 'I believe that, as a Politburo Member, I did not realise to the full and in a truly principled way the main danger for perestroika, specifically, the planned and ever more active work of anti-socialist forces aimed at weakening and, eventually, destroying from inside the Communist Party and the socialist Union of republics'.

By the time this was stated by Ligachev, a bitter inner-party struggle had erupted. The advancement of the 28th Party Congress by nearly a year presaged this. This inner party struggle centred on the party in the Russian republic, which had 56 per cent of the total membership. It took place in a situation where the crisis for the Party was building up with the growth of national chauvinism and splits in the republics within the CPSU. It is necessary to devote some attention to these two aspects, which had a decisive impact on the future of the Party.

NATIONAL CHAUVINISM: THE PARTY OVERWHELMED

A major hallmark of the Gorbachevian reforms was the total underestimation of the potential of nationality and ethnic conflicts and rise of national chauvinism. As early as 1986 the removal of G. Aliyev from the Secretaryship of the Uzbekistan Central Committee sparked off mass demonstrations in Alma Ata. These were the first mass political demonstrations and they were in protest against the ouster of Aliyev. This was followed by the conflict between Uzbekistan and Armenia over the Nagomy-Karabakh enclave. The third transcauscasian republic, Georgia, soon followed with its own nationalist-separatist movement. Over in the Baltic republics, the separatist nationalist forces gathered momentum.

But the energy displayed in 'reorganizing' the Party Politburo and Central apparatus seems to have taken up all the time of the Gorbachevian leadership. Later Gorbachev was to confess that he could not foresee the rise of such forces and the damage they would do. In the republics where the Party faced the offensive of the national-separatist forces, the central leadership could give no firm guidance and support. Instead they were being advised publicly and in Party forums to encourage glasnost, to let these forces vilify the Party and defame the past. Virulent nationalist propaganda was to be protected in the name of glasnost. The Soviet media highlighted historical wrongs and injustices and denounced the CPSU handling of the nationalities question. At no point did Gorbachev and the Central leadership give a call to all Communists and to units to combat these forces politically and organizationally.

After the virus of national chauvinism invaded the Party in many republics and imminent danger of splits loomed ahead, only then a weak effort was made. 'We should also reaffirm today that membership in the Communist Party is incompatible with nationalism and chauvinism', reported Gorbachev. 'Vladimir Lenin created the Bolshevik Party as an internationalist Party in spirit, programme and ethnic makeup.' (*Report by M. Gorbachev to CPSU*, Central Committee Plenary meeting 29 July 1989).

The September 1989 Central Committee Plenary adopted a Platform of Nationalities which though well intentioned, could not be put into practice as matters had gone too far ahead. The first crisis came on the separation of the Lithuanian Communist Party. In December 1989, the 20th Congress of the Communist Party of Lithuania passed by a majority the 'Declaration of Independence of the Communist Party of Lithuania'. With the new statutes, programme and rules it declared that 'the programme and rules of the CPSU are no longer valid for the units of the Lithuanian Party'.

The Central Committee of the CPSU was convened to discuss the Lithuanian Party's action. In his report 'The destiny of Perestroika lies in Party unity', Gorbachev revealed that there were two opinions within the leadership. One was for accepting the *fait accompli* and that developments should be allowed to take their course. The other was very critical and felt the future of the Party and Soviet state was at stake. The second opinion suggested that the Lithuanian Party should be disbanded and all Communists registered anew. The functions of the Lithuanian Central Committee could be temporarily fulfilled by an organizing Committee, which should be materially and organizationally supported by the Central Committee.

Gorbachev said both 'has its logic and shortcomings'. He did not adopt the latter course. His intentions were clear. 'We proceed from the assumption that the independence of the republican Communist parties is possible and desirable within the framework of the CPSU, as the sovereignty of republics is possible and desirable within a renewed federation', said Gorbachev.

This was a major concession and departure from democratic centralism. The independence of the republican Communist parties is equated with the sovereignty of the republics in a federation. This acknowledged that the republican parties could function within a federal setup of the CPSU. With this outlook, it is not surprising that the balkanization of the Party on ethnic lines proceeded speedily.

By the end of 1989 and beginning 1990, the Communist

parties in the three Caucasian republics were in full retreat in the face of the nationalist attacks. De facto power was in the hands of the Popular Front in Armenia, the round table of separatists in Georgia and the Popular Front in Azerbaijan.

The warning Gorbachev gave in July 1989 became a mockery, 'There can be no excuse for a Communist who has adopted the positions of chauvinism or nationalism. In point of fact, this position is a departure from one of the most important political principles of the Party'. With his compromise with the 'national Communists', Gorbachev ensured that the floodgates be opened which overwhelmed the CPSU.

INNER-PARTY STRUGGLE INTENSIFIES

The developments on the nationalities front with its shattering effects on the Party led to the demand for the constitution of the Communist Party of the Russian Federation as a separate unit. Up till then, the Russian Communists had no separate organizational structure and worked under the CPSU Central Committee directly.

The February 1990 Central Committee Plenum decided that the process of forming such a Russian organizational unit should begin. As a run up to the 28th Congress of the CPSU the Russian Federation Party Conference was held in June 1990. This event was looked upon with trepidation by the 'liberals', the Yeltsin supporters and the Democratic Platform, as they saw the formation of such a unit as the consolidation of the 'hardliners' or the conservatives as they called those opposed to the gamut of reforms.

The Congress saw a blistering attack on the leadership of the CPSU. The dominant mood was summed up by the first speaker to take the floor after Gorbachev had delivered his report. Ivan Osadchiy, member of the Preparatory Committee of the Russian Party Conference presented the second report. He said 'many communists were convinced that the CPSU leadership was guilty for the Party was put in the position of one who had to catch up, consequently was losing initiative all the time, and cannot properly influence the development of events'. In a telling indictment, he blamed the CPSU leadership which had reduced the Party 'to crouching unarmed in the trenches under massive shelling by anti-socialist forces, which have rapidly organized themselves'. Osadchiy spoke out against turning the Russian Communist Party into 'a social democratic, reformist party of the parliamentary type'. The majority of Communists are convinced that 'only a Communist Party of the Leninist type, based on Leninist foundations' can pull Russia out of its crisis.

TASS observed, 'The position, set out by the representative of the Preparatory Committee, seemed to be well received by many delegates. There was a storm of applause as he was leaving the rostrum'.

The Congress also saw the clash of opinions between the representatives of the Marxist Platform and the Democratic Platform. Another representative of the Initiative Congress of the Russian Communist Party, which held two meetings in Leningrad, Viktor Tiulkin, demanded an alternative to the policy which 'had given nothing to the people over the past five perestroika years'. He said new perestroika dogmas had replaced the old dogmas. He cited the Party's rejection of the class approach as an instrument for analysing social phenomena as leading to a shift in objectives. He concluded by stating the stand of the Leningrad conference that 'we favour the unity of Marxists, not the unity of Marxists and those who pervert Marxism'.

The Conference of the Russian Federation saw determined

opposition to the course of the leadership manifesting as the dominant trend. It was the first and only organized resistance to the Gorbachevian reforms to be expressed in the Party in the six years of perestroika.

PLATFORMS WITHIN THE PARTY

The February 1990 Central Committee plenum while finalizing the Draft Platform had decided to allow communists to band together to present alternative platforms. As a result thc Dcmocratic Platform which wanted the Parry to take to social democracy and become a parliamentary party emerged; the other trend, the Marxist Platform was critical of the direction of perestroika reforms and wanted guarantees that they will remain within the socialist framework while eliminating bureaucracy and revamping the economic and political structure; there were also the Working People's Platform which drew on the ideas of the congresses of the United Front of the Working People held in 1989 and 1990 and the Leningrad Initiative Committee which were strongly critical of the leadership's abandonment of working class positions.

The Russian Party Conference went ahead with the election of its Central Committee and General Secretary despite the advice of Gorbachev and the central leadership to postpone this till after the 28th Congress. The Russian Party Conference was seen as a dire threat by the Yeltsinites and the Democratic Platform. They branded it as a 'conservative show'. Some members in Moscow, particularly in the media, dropped out of the Party or refused to pay dues. The Moscow Party Secretary Prokofiev was with the 'democratic' trend and he made it clear that his city unit was not in agreement with the majority positions of the Congress. Those adhering to the Democratic Platform from Russia were clear about splitting away but decided to wait for the 28th Congress before finalizing their stand.

PERVERSION OF IDEOLOGY

Gorbachev had waxed eloquent about the ideological role of the Party at the 27th Congress. Later he talked of breaking new ideological ground in bringing about a 'humane and democratic socialism'. But the ideological remoulding which went on under his leadership bred and nurtured ideas hostile to socialism and to Marxism. Nothing else can explain the outlook which crept into the top echelons of the Party. In 1990, Alexander Tsipko wrote an article which questioned the very necessity of the October Revolution and traced the roots of Stalinism to Marxism. Such writings had become a common occurrence in the Soviet press but what made this piece unusual was that it was written by a person who was in the ideological department of the Central Committee of the CPSU. Tsipko later on brazenly announced to the press that he would remain in the Party till the 28th Congress and if the Party failed to change itself, he would quit it.

This was only the logical conclusion of the drive to denigrate the socialist past initiated by the Gorbachevian leadership. Even the evaluation of the positive features of the seventy years of socialism made by Gorbachev in the 70th October Revolution Anniversary report in November 1987 was abandoned by the leadership. Glorification of social democracy became the norm. Yakovlev on the eve of the 28th Congress stated in *Pravda*, 'We must rediscover social democracy for ourselves'. Touching upon the possibility of the convergence of the two social systems, Yakovlev said 'it was an objective process, it had been going on for a long time and will be gaining momentum'.

Eduard Shevernadze who championed 'universal human values' as the Foreign Minister declared in the 28th Congress that he saw nothing wrong with the developments in Eastern Europe. He said from the rostrum of the Congress, 'Soviet diplomacy has not set, nor could it set the aim of opposing the elimination in other countries of the administrative – command system and totalitarian regimes that has been imposed on them and are alien to them'. He welcomed the dismantling of the GDR terming the split of Germany 'artificial and unnatural'.

Aleksandr Yakovlev, his colleague in the Politburo and another trusted voice of Gorbachev also declared that the issue of German unification had been 'raised by life itself'. He purveyed the illusion that 'a new peaceful period in the life of humanity has begun and the constitution of a new civilization of a new type without wars and arms is being started'. A few months later, the world witnessed the vicious Gulf War begun by the US and its allies against Iraq.

Objectively a major section of the CPSU leadership reached the same positions as Boris Yeltsin. As a member of the Central Committee, Yeltsin visited the USA in 1987 and praised capitalism and called communism 'a pie in the sky'. The Party Central Committee did not act against Yeltsin then, nor it did take any action against the Yakovlevs, Shevernadzes and Tsipkos. This shows the total ideological disarray which came about in the leadership of the CPSU with one section openly out to destroy the Marxist-Leninist ideological basis of the Party.

It is this outlook which directly aided the pro-capitalist forces and encouraged them to oust the socialist system in Eastern Europe.

The trio which left the Politburo – Shevernadze, Yakovlev and Medvedev (who was in charge of ideology) – at the 28th Congress played an instrumental role in disarming the CPSU and destroying its political-organizational basis.

They enjoyed the patronage and support of Gorbachev. With their crass admiration for social democracy, craven subservience to American susceptibilities and contempt for their country's socialist past they were the hatchet men for the demolition job. Shevernadze, the pet favourite of the Bush administration, wrecked the foundations of Soviet foreign policy and took pride in this; Yakovlev originated many of the social democratic ideas to revamp the Party's programme and Medvedev supervized the ideological liquidation. With such a leadership, a coup took place within the Party.

The 28th Congress held in July 1990 after discussions adopted the Draft Platform which was now called the Policy statement, 'For a humane and democratic socialism'. For the first time a programmatic document of the Party deleted the term 'Marxism-Leninism' as the ideological basis of the Party; it made no reference to imperialism as a category, presumably it had also ceased to exist; there is no reference to class struggles around the world or support to the international working class movement. The adoption of this policy statement was a major departure from the basic Marxist outlook. Various ideas alien to a working class party were accepted.

THE 28TH CONGRESS

The 28th Congress could not resolve the basic questions. There were sharp differences of opinion and heated debates in the Commissions. The Congress saw an intense struggle on the question of democratic centralism. In the draft platform presented to the February Central Committee the reaffirmation of democratic centralism was absent. Many in the Central Committee demanded its inclusion and Gorbachev announced in the press conference that the Central Committee did not favour the deletion of democratic centralism. The draft platform had stated that 'there is a need for rethinking of the principle of democratic centralism'. But the final policy statement still did not directly affirm adherence to this Leninist principle. It spoke of the need 'for resolutely rejecting democratic centralism the way it took shape in the conditions of command and administrative system and rigid centralization'. Coupled with the freedom for different platforms to indulge in factional mobilization and the failure to enforce discipline on a number of leading personalities who violated the collective understanding and decisions, the way was opened for the abandonment of democratic centralism.

Another point of conflict was the arrangement introduced by Gorbachev in the 19th Conference that secretaries of Party committees should serve as Chairpersons of Soviets. As per the working group which discussed the relations between the Party and the Soviets, 'Heated debates on having secretaries of the Party committees to serve simultaneously as Chairman of Soviets at all levels failed to narrow differences of opinion'.

The 28th Congress saw the formal renunciation of membership by Boris Yeltsin. He walked out in the latter part of the Congress after his demands to change the name of the Party and to convert it into a parliamentary party were rejected. Along with him some of the Democratic Platform group also left the Party.

At the 28th Congress, Gorbachev understood that it was difficult to 'restructure' the party out of its Leninist mould. He said despairingly at the Congress, 'And now we are talking about a crisis in the Party. Its roots are none than the inability, and in a number of cases unwillingness to understand we are living in a new society'. Earlier he had told the delegates, 'From the atmosphere of the Congress, from many speeches and the methods of debating used by some delegates, I sensed that not everyone by any means has understood that the Party is living and working in a difficult society, that a different Party, a renewed one, with a different style of work is needed'.

Only Gorbachev's concept of a renewed Party was not the Leninist type of which he talked about in 1986, but a party of the social democratic type. Only the threat of a split in the Party circumscribed his drive to that goal. The Gorbachevian clique from then on began in right earnest to marginalize and bypass the Party. For this it still needed to control the levers of leadership. The period July 1990 to July 1991 – a fateful year – saw the rapid decline of the Party, disorganized from the top. The departure from the Politburo of people like Shevernadze, Yakovlev and Medvedev did not mark any break from the perilous direction the Party was set on. Their abandoning the Party leadership was only the advance portents of a sinking ship.

THE FINAL BOUT IN THE PARTY

The bitter struggle continued within. The main target of the bourgeois liberalizers was now the so-called conservative leadership of the party in the Russian federation. One of the leaders of the Democratic Russia group Rutskoi joined hands with Yeltsin and became his Vice Presidential candidate for the June Presidential elections to the Russian Republic. Along with him a group deserted. The Russian Party was split by these bourgeois reformers before the July 1991 Central Committee Plenum. The struggle to preserve the unity of the party led to the resignation of Polozkov as Secretary who was elected just a year before at the first Congress.

The final blow was sought to be delivered by Yeltsin after his victory in the Presidential elections in June. His decree banning Party units in work places and the security forces came in mid-July. It was a pre-emptive strike to disable the Party. Gorbachev kept quiet for a full week despite repeated calls by Party committees and leaders to declare this decree illegal. It was only in the July Central Committee Plenum that he was forced to accept a resolution condemning the Yeltsin decree. Yet he did not use his Presidential powers to render the decree illegal.

The July 1991 Central Committee meeting was held in a tense atmosphere. In the earlier April meeting, there was strong criticism of Gorbachev's positions leading to his threat of resigning from the general secretaryship. By the time of the July meeting, Gorbachev had lost the confidence of a substantial part of the Party. It is reported that 40 regional party committees sent resolutions demanding his resignation. The Communist Initiative Conference of Communists in the Russian Republic demanded that he step down. It was widely expected that the renewed demand would make his position untenable in the July meeting. But this time there was no such pressure. A plausible explanation has been given by Roy Medvedev, a supporter of Gorbachev at that time. He thought the onslaught did not take place because of Yeltsin's attack on the Party by the ban decree. The Central Committee members against Gorbachev decided that the threat from Yeltsin would have to be met first.

The July Central Committee decided to call yet another Congress by November-December 1991. The meeting adopted a draft programme which met with only minimal opposition in the voting. This draft took a qualitative leap in carrying forward the CPSU to social democracy. The draft which was published on 8 August did not talk of any of the basic concepts of Marxism-Leninism; in fact it refutes the relevance of class struggle in the contemporary world and speaks of Marxism as only one of the sources of ideological inspiration for the Party.

The twelve months after the 28th Congress inexorably led to the events in August 1991. The CPSU ceased to be a Party unified on the basis of democratic centralism. The Congress had conceded independence to the Republican parties in the policy statement and rules. One by one the Party units in the republics – Georgia, Armenia, Uzbekistan, Kazakhstan – went down in the face of the rising national chauvinism and the abandonment of the centralized line by the Gorbachevian leadership. The Union Treaty secretly negotiated bypassed the Party and for that matter the Supreme Soviet. Its proposed signing on 20 August sparked off the abortive attempt to halt it on 19 August. What was unexpected was the feeble and half-hearted effort to take power. Those who initiated the take-over were precisely those whom Gorbachev had to take into the leading positions in the Government and Security Council under the pressure of the sections of the Party which refused to buy the bourgeois liberal line.

Gorbachev crossed the Rubicon on 23 August 1991. Returning to Moscow after the failure of the takeover, he made a feeble attempt on 22 August to defend the Party and the Communists. But the next day he capitulated under Yeltsin's merciless pressure. He endorsed the decision to illegalize the Party, announced his resignation from the General Secretaryship and recommended the dissolution of the Central Committee. This marked the final act – Gorbachev himself became the instrument for the dissolution of the Party.

CAUSES FOR THE DOWNFALL

The tragedy for the CPSU came in a dual form. Firstly there were the decades of theory and practice which ossified the Party. The merger of Party and government functions gradually made the Party part of the establishment, robbing it of its capacity to work and organize as a political force which earns its vanguard role amongst the working class and the people. The growth and consolidation of bureaucratism, the maintenance of Party privileges and inability to correctly assess the negative phenomenon in society including the nationality-ethnic problems – alienated the people from the Party to a substantial degree.

The 1985-86 period saw the first concrete attempts to grapple with these problems. That is why Gorbachev's reforms seemed a potent vehicle for rejuvenating the Party revitalizing socialism. This promise was grossly betrayed.

Secondly, what could have been a process of reform and rectification on Marxist-Leninist lines for strengthening socialism soon became its opposite. The CPSU itself became a contributory factor to this retrograde progress.

The drive for bourgeois-liberal reforms found support from within the ranks of the Party. Such a response stemmed from the strata of technocrats, intellectuals and managerial personnel within the Party. They were eager to garner the benefits of a liberal-capitalist regime by breaking away from socialism. Already privileged, they were envious of the standards of living of the Western elites and aspired to enjoy them. It is this strata which fuelled the reforms to move away from Marxism. Many of the leading personnel now aiding Yeltsin or Gavril Popiov and A. Sobchak, the Mayors of Moscow and Leningrad, are all drawn from the ranks of the CPSU.

The CPI(M) in its August 1988 Central Committee resolution which spelt out the framework for analysing the Soviet developments had warned,

> But it has to be understood and underlined sharply that all such measures will strengthen society if the guiding role of the Marxism-Leninism is preserved and the role of the Party as a leading force of society as vanguard of the working class is ensured. Without these latter two conditions new measures would not realise the socialist initiative of the masses and ensure their participation in running the state.

The CPI(M) stated this with the experience of China in mind. There two successive general secretaries of the Party in the process of initiating reform sought to undermine the Party's leading role and make basic departures from the framework of socialism. Precisely, what was warned against, happened. The CPSU step by step was guided by its leadership to adopt positions outside the framework of Marxism-Leninism; by 1989-90 it had also lost the will to be a vanguard force and its leadership worked to abolish any changes for maintaining its leading role.

The retreat from Marxism-Leninism, seen from the 70th anniversary report of Gorbachev, culminated in the virtual acceptance of social democracy in the Draft programme adopted in July 1991 by the Central Committee plenary. The Party in an unprincipled manner allowed the concentration of all powers in an individual in the 19th All Union Conference in June 1988. The Party surrendered to the challenge of national chauvinism in 1989. The Party decided to reduce itself to one of the many parties in a multi-party system in the February 1990 Central Committee Plenum. And finally, organizationally, though it had not formally abandoned democratic centralism the CPSU had by 1990 done away with its essence in inner-party functioning.

The quick denouncement of these events in a space of four years sealed the fate of the Party. When the counter-revolutionary offensive spearheaded by Yeltsin took place in August – the 15 million Communists who still remained in the CPSU were a disoriented lot, bombarded by bourgeois ideology from within its ranks; sharply divided on nationality – ethnic lines; bitter at the betrayal of its leadership and unable to organizationally maintain their cohesion.

Without Marxism-Leninism, a Communist Party ceases to have a revolutionary theory. Without democratic centralism, it cannot remain a revolutionary organization. When the CPSU leadership abandoned both, the Party of Lenin ceased to exist in its original basic form and character.

This proved fatal for the socialist system and the Soviet Union us a federation which were both products of the October Revolution.

ECONOMY: REFORMS FOR RESTORATION OF CAPITALISM (1991)

Sitaram Yechury

The systematic dismantling of the socialist economic foundations is one of the key factors leading to the collapse of socialism and the beginning of the process of restoration of capitalism in the USSR. During the course of the six years of perestroika, many important questions have been raised. Why did the relative economic stagnation set in by the end of the seventies? Was this due only to the distortions of the past? Was it, therefore, inevitable that socialism was bound to collapse sometime or the other? Was there any other way of restructuring the economy while preserving socialism? These, along with many theoretical and ideological questions, challenge the revolutionary tenets of Marxism-Leninism and the historical experience of socialism. We here confine ourselves to the study of the various measures taken under perestroika by the Gorbachev leadership and the restructuring of the socialist economic relations to show that the collapse of socialism in the USSR, is due in the main, to the systematic dismantling of the socialist economic foundations. These six years have in fact been a period of intense class struggle, with the triumph of the counter-revolutionary forces for the time being. It is, therefore, necessary for communists all over the world to try and understand how this has been possible.

I

It would be an understatement to state that the Soviet economy today is in shambles. Within a span of six years, this once mighty economic bulwark against imperialism has been reduced to utter chaos and anarchy. The gross industrial output growth rate was 4.4 per cent in 1986. While it is difficult to estimate today, the *Financial Times* places it anywhere between (-) 8.8 to (-) 20 per cent of 1991. Despite bumper harvests in 1986 and 1987, the Soviet Union is today importing over 40 million tonnes of food grains. In 1987, Gorbachev himself had to acknowledge that the USSR was producing over 200 million tonnes of food grains. This is more than the production of the entire European community of nations who have a larger population than that of the Soviet Union. The per capita consumption and production was higher in the USSR than in Europe. In 1991, however, there is talk of hunger and starvation.

The Financial Times describes the current situation as marked by a hyper-inflation of 7 per cent a week, a drastic fall in the coal reserves and an impending foreign debt crisis. During these six years, the foreign debt almost doubled to nearly 70 billion US dollars, while the Budget deficit grew by more than 600 per cent reaching over 300 billion roubles in 1991. The USSR is reportedly importing paper to print currency needs. The social security provisions guaranteed by socialism have disintegrated. Food shortages are without precedent worse even from the war period. The prices have shot up to such a level that even those with steady incomes are unable to make both ends meet. Unemployment is rapidly rising, and hunger and deprivation, unknown to generations of Soviet citizens, has begun to rapidly surface.

II

Before studying this tragic dismantling of the socialist economic foundations it is necessary to note in brief certain objective circumstances under which the Bolshevik Revolution triumphed. The draft resolution on ideological issues released for the 14th CPI (M) Congress states:

Marx and Engels had projected the triumph of world socialism as the post-capitalist stage in human evolution. The process of this world-wide transformation was conceived of on the basis of the overthrow of capitalism in at least some of the major capitalistically developed countries, to begin with. The maturing of capitalism to the stage of imperialism and the sharpening of its inherent world contradictions, however permitted the possibility of breaking the imperialist chain of world bondage at its weakest link. The Russian working class under Lenin's leadership, applying the inviolable Marxist tool of 'concrete analysis of concrete conditions' converted this possibility into an epoch making reality.

However, socialist revolutions triumphed in countries that were capitalistically the least developed and relatively backward. The absence of a triumphant revolution in any advanced capitalist country by itself imposed limitations on these countries to consolidate socialism. The relatively low level of productive forces and the associated backward production and social relations had to be substantially raised, and at a breakneck speed, bypassing the stage of capitalism, to levels that could sustain socialist construction. This had to be done relying purely on internal resources, without access to the higher techniques of production developed by capitalism and in an hostile international atmosphere when world capitalism tried all methods at its disposal to asphyxiate socialism. It is in fact a testimony to the superiority of the socialist system that such a gigantic task could be achieved.

Lenin was acutely conscious of these limitations. In fact, he was constantly attempting the process of socialist construction with various experiments. The New Economic Policy was one such, and not, as many like to argue today, the fundamental blueprint of what should be the pattern of socialist economic construction. In one of his unfinished works, *Economics and*

Politics in the Era of the Dictatorship of the Proletariat, he notes,

> Theoretically, there can be no doubt that between capitalism and communism there lies a definite transition period which must combine the feature and properties of both these forms of social economy. This transition period has to be a period of struggle between dying capitalism and nascent communism – or, in other words, between capitalism which has been defeated but not destroyed and communism which has been born but is still very feeble.
>
> In Russia, the dictatorship of the proletariat must inevitably differ in certain particulars from what it would be in the advanced countries, owing to the very great backwardness and petty-bourgeois character of our country. But the basic forces – and the basic forms of social economy – are the same in Russia as in any capitalist country, so that the pecularities can apply only to what is of lesser importance.
>
> The basic forms of social economy are capitalism, petty commodity production, and communism. The basic forces are the bourgeoisie, the petty bourgeoisie (the peasantry in particular) and the proletariat.
>
> The economic system of Russia in the era of the dictatorship of the proletariat represents the struggle of labour, united on communist principles on the scale of a vast state and making its first steps – the struggle against petty commodity production and against the capitalism which still persists and against that which is newly arising on the basis of the petty commodity production.

Emphasizing the need to replace petty-commodity producing peasant farming by large farms organized by the workers state as the essence of socialist economic construction Lenin warns that, in petty-commodity production, 'we have an extremely broad and a very sound deep-rooted basis for capitalism, a basis on which capitalism persists or arises anew in a bitter struggle against communism. The forms of this struggle are private speculation and profiteering versus state procurement of grain (and other products) and state distribution of products in general.' Indeed, this turned out to be prophetic 70 years later, as we shall see later. Perestroika encouraged privatization. Speculation, trading and profiteering grew at a stunning pace under the guise of cooperatives. Hoarding and artificial shortages sabotaged the 'State distribution of products'. In the process, even the bourgeois press admits, new Soviet millionaires emerged arising 'anew in a bitter struggle against Communism'.

Asserting that socialism means the abolition of classes, Lenin identifies two necessary factors, 'First, overthrow of the land owners and capitalists', the second which he considers more difficult, 'to abolish difference between factory workers and peasant and to make workers all of them'. Lenin then describes this task as being 'incomparably more difficult and will of necessity take a long time. It is not a problem that can be solved by overthrowing a class. It can be solved only by the organizational reconstruction of the whole social economy, by a transition from individual, dis-united, petty commodity production to large-scale social production. This transition must of necessity be extremely protracted. It may only be delayed and complicated by hasty and incautious administrative and legislative measures. It can be accelerated only by affording such assistance to the peasant as will enable him to effect an immense improvement in his whole farming technique, to reform it radically.' Then Lenin goes on,

> In order to solve the second and most difficult part of the problem, the proletariat, after having defeated the bourgeoisie,

> must unswervingly conduct its policy towards the peasantry along the following fundamental lines. The proletariat must separate, demarcate the working peasant from the peasant owner, the peasant worker from the peasant huckster, the peasant who labours from the peasant who profiteers. In this demarcation lies the whole essence of socialism.

Such demarcation, however, Lenin states: 'is an extremely difficult one because in real life all the features of the *peasant*, however diverse they may be, however, contradictory they may be, are fused into one whole'.

Unfortunately, the Soviet Union was not allowed to construct the socialist economy without any interference from the outside world. Socialism was not permitted the luxury to patiently transform the petty commodity producing peasant economy into a Socialist one by employing the 'demarcation' that Lenin talked of. Capitalist armed intervention, the Civil War, the encirclement, the growing certainty of a world war, all these demanded, for the very survival of socialism, that the pace of socialist construction be quickened. This necessitated the collectivization drive and in the process many distortions occurred concerning the 'demarcation' that Lenin talked off. Even Stalin in 'Dizzy with success' had noted some problems.

Even the worst critics of Stalin, cannot but admit that minus collectivization, the Soviet Union could not have sustained the war or defeated the Nazi army. It could not have successfully rebuilt its war ravaged economy at an amazing speed in five years.

Despite the distortions and excesses, which in no way can be condoned, even Gorbachev had to admit that collectivization, made possible for peasantry 'to become a modern civilized class of society'. He in fact says, 'Even many of the objective students of this period of history do not seem to be able to grasp the importance, need and inevitability of collectivization in our country'. This was in 1987, in his book, *Perestroika.*

It is on the basis of such solid economic foundations – State ownership of the means of production in industry, large scale social production in agriculture based on State-owned, collective and cooperative farming, integrated together by Central Planning – that the Soviet Union could emerge as a mighty economic and military bulwark against imperialism. This, it must be noted, is despite the tremendous drain of resources away from economic activity designed to increase peoples' welfare, imposed by imperialism through the nuclear arms race. Added to this, is the great internationalist duty that the USSR performed in materially aiding the national liberation struggles and the economies of the newly independent ex-colonies.

The USSR emerged not only as an economic bulwark against imperialism but had guaranteed to its citizens social and economic rights hitherto unknown in human civilization, rights of employment, food, shelter, health, education, day-care, old age – rights which today even in the most advanced capitalist countries are not granted in the universal sense to every individual. All this was possible only on the basis of a gigantic people's effort.

III

Relative Stagnation

By mid-1970s however the Soviet economy showed declining trends in growth rates. This is for the first time since the introduction of the five-year plan that such a trend becomes visible. During the decade 1976 to 1985 the growth rates of both the national product and industrial production declined. The plan targets were not achieved under the five-year plan of 1976-80 and 1981-85. In the earlier plan agricultural production grew at 1.16 per cent and the latter at 2.1 per cent, but both fell well short of the plan targets.

It is this situation that confronted the Soviet economy during the last days of the Brezhnev period. It was in fact Andropov who, succeeding Brezhnev, identified and spoke of the need for revitalizing the Soviet economy in order to overcome the relative stagnation. In a refreshing theoretical contribution on the occasion of Marx's death centenary in 1983, Andropov says,

> One may repeat again and again Marx's basic idea that to speed up progress of the productive forces one must have the corresponding forms of organization of economic life, but no progress will be made until this theoretical truth is translated into the concrete language of practice. The cornerstone task being put forward today is that of carefully considering and consistently carrying out measures that can give full scope for the action of the enormous creative forces inherent in our economy. These measures must be thoroughly prepared and be realistic, and this means that when working them out one must undeviatingly proceed from the laws governing the development of the economic system of socialism. The objective character of these laws makes it necessary to be rid of any attempts to guide the economy by methods alien to its nature . . . The efficiency of the socialist national economy should be judged, of course, not only by purely economic criteria but also by social ones, with account taken of the ultimate goal of social production. Under capitalism such a goal is profit on capital; under socialism – as was proved theoretically by Marx – it is the welfare of the working people and the creation of conditions for all-round development of the individual. Existing socialism clothes this tenet of Marx's theory in living flesh.

Subsequently, speaking to the CPSU Central Committee Plenary Session Andropov says in June 1983,

> It is well known that the make-up of every society is determined in the long run by the level of development of its productive forces, by the nature and state of production relations. In our social development we have now approached such a point in history at which deep qualitative changes in productive forces and a corresponding perfection of production relations have not only ripened but have also become inevitable. This is not just our wish, comrades, this is an objective necessity and there is no way of avoiding it . . . . The key task in the economic sphere is the cardinal improvement of labour productivity. Here we must strive to attain the highest world level. For, with good reason, Lenin regarded this as in the long run the most important, the main thing for the victory of the new social system. This task acquired special importance now, in the context of the scientific and technological revolution, both for our domestic development and in the international aspect . . . The main way to a qualitative shift in productive forces is, of course, the transition to intensive development, the merging in reality of the advantages of our socialist system with the achievements of the scientific and technological revolution, of moreover, its latest stage which promises dramatic technological changes in many spheres of production.

The western capitalist media, forever antagonistic to socialism, had projected Gorbachev as the messiah for having identified the relative stagnation in the Soviet economy. In their urge to blame the socialist past for the present situation they ignored the theoretical and practical considerations drawn up by the CPSU Central Committee for revitalizing the socialist economy.

The CPSU Central Committee Plenary session of April

1985 marking the ascendancy of Gorbachev as the General Secretary of the CPSU had declared the necessity 'to accelerate the country's social and economic development, to resolutely overcome the unfavourable tendencies in the economy, impart proper paramountcy to it, open scope for initiative and creativity of the masses, for truly revolutionary transformation of society'.

27th Congress: Correct Analysis

Subsequently, the 27th Congress of the CPSU in 1986 gave a theoretical basis for the need to change the methods of economic management corresponding to the developing social productive forces. Under socialism when social production grows at a tremendous pace, the methods of economic management have to constantly improve and adapt to these. These are objective laws of socialist political economy. For instance, it is possible at a certain point to increase the levels of agricultural production by bringing all available land under cultivation. Once this phase is over, further growth in production will have to be based on increasing the productivity of both labour and land, through improved methods and technology. Likewise, industry which can to a certain point develop on the basis of available natural resources and raw materials, will have to constantly upgrade the production process technologically, in order to maintain and increase the levels of production and productivity. This constant increase in productivity based on technology especially the productivity of labour, is a sphere in which Lenin had stated socialism would have to surpass capitalism. In other words, as social productive forces develop, the methods of economic management will have to change from those of 'extensive' to 'intensive' development.

If such changes are not made in the proper time then not only will socialism's full potential be not realised, but it would also lead to a phase of relative economic stagnation. This in turn, would create a situation where people's aspirations are not completely met. The consequent dissatisfaction, amongst other factors, in an international atmosphere of consumerist capitalist propaganda, creates the breeding ground for people's alienation and growth of anti-socialist ideas.

Correctly identifying the problems, the 27th Congress report adopted the strategy of accelerating the economic development to break from this relative stagnation. Its report says, 'What do we mean by acceleration? First of all raising the rate of economic growth. But that is not all. In substance it means a new quality of growth and all out intensification of production on the basis of scientific and technological progress, a structural reconstruction of the economy, effective forms for management and of organizing and stimulating labour'.

Perestroika or economic reforms are summarized in the following words, 'socialist economic acceleration and the consolidation of socialism in practice should be the supreme criteria in the improvement of management and the entire system of socialist production relations'.

Thus, we see during this period since 1983, including the first two years of Gorbachev's leadership, a serious effort being made by the CPSU to overcome the relative economic stagnation which was caused by the failure to make timely changes in the methods of economic management as the productive forces rapidly developed in the earlier decades.

However, soon after the 27th Party Congress, one could see a significant shift in the perceptions for the cause of this economic stagnation. Perestroika's twin brother, glasnost had provided the umbrella under whose shade the anti-socialist forces grew unchecked. What needs to be stressed is that instead of pinpointing the concrete changes that had to be brought about to correct the delays in changes in economic management, the economic stagnation was in fact ideologically laid at the doorstep of past history. The gigantic socialist construction that we refer to above was in fact stated as the reason for the present economic stagnation. What initially therefore started as reforms to strengthen socialism snowballed rapidly during the two years following the 27th Congress into a war-cry against socialism itself.

Cooperatives

In 1987, the CPSU Central Committee circulated a new law on state enterprises, which after substantial debate was adopted in January 1988. This law according to Gorbachev 'has provided cooperatives with the truly golden key to the organization of their activities. The necessary conditions are today being created in practice for equivalent exchange and effective cooperation between State and cooperative enterprises.' Speaking to the 4th All-Union Conference of Collective Farmers in March 1988, Gorbachev states 'in over one year alone almost 14,000 cooperatives have been set up and began functioning in this country in consumer goods production and processing of secondary raw materials.' These supposedly employed over 1.5 lakh people. Thus came into existence, a system of private employment. In a situation of full employment under socialism, the cooperatives could hire labour power only by offering wages higher than those offered by the state. Thus, the fundamental characteristic of capitalist production – that of hiring labour power, the generation of surplus value and thus appropriation by the cooperatives as profit – was endorsed and came into effect by 1988. Such cooperatives mushroomed in large numbers. According to official Soviet statistics by 1 January 1989, the number of cooperatives grew to 77,500, by 1 July 1989 this rose to

133,000 and by 1 October 1989 it rose to 171,500. By the end of 1989 the number of people engaged in the cooperatives stood at 4.5 million.

Far from engaging in any increase in the production capacity of the economy, most of these cooperatives were classified under the term consumer services. It is clear that what they were engaging in was not actual production but trade in terms of buying materials from the state enterprises and outlets and reselling them with 'consumer services'. On the one hand, this led to rapid inflation and on the other led to disappearance of many consumer goods from the state shops.

Ironically, even Gorbachev in October 1988 had to bemoan that 'a kind of public has turned up which, in point of fact has obtained, in the name of the cooperatives an opportunity to legalize its illegal incomes and acquisitions in a dishonest way. And now it almost seems that they are going to flourish . . .'

Despite all the pious resolutions of the Supreme Soviet in enforcing laws against such practices, these flourished and became the main source of primary accumulation of capital. Thus, creating in an embryonic form, a social exploiting class that was eliminated decades ago in the Soviet Union. These provided the social base for the anti-socialist forces, which under the guise of intellectuals and academicians had been arguing for the creation of a 'full-fledged market economy', in other words, restoration of capitalism.

Ironically, all this was done by invoking Lenin and his concept of socialism as a 'free association of producers'.

Changes in Relations of Production

This process of the systematic dismantling of the socialist economic foundations and the restoration of capitalist relations was ideologically propped up by offering capitalist prescriptions to socialist problems. This is best contained in the plan produced by the academician Shatalin for the complete restoration of capitalist relations in the Soviet Union. 'Humanity has not yet developed anything more efficient than a market economy', he wrote. 'The prerequisite to ensure the effective functioning of the market includes *de jure* equality of all types of property including private property. Revenue from property should be recognized as lawful profit.'

Such an unashamed advocacy of the exploitative capitalist order had to be based on proving that the socialist economic system was inefficient, on the one hand, and by invoking socialist experience itself to show the supremacy of the market over the foundations of the centrally planned economy. Both these tasks were admirably done by the Soviet academicians, who on the one hand, debunked the Soviet working class, and on the other, constantly invoked Lenin's new economic policy as the only blueprint for socialist economic construction.

Taking sustenance from Gorbachev's and the CPSU's strong criticism about the parasitic tendencies of certain sections of the working class, these academicians argued for unemployment justifying and in fact extolling unemployment. Placing the entire blame of the economic stagnation on the inefficiency of the Soviet working class, these academicians, such as Nikolai Shmelyov, state with the characteristic contempt of a petty bourgeois intellectual against the working class, 'We must not close our eyes to the economic harm that results from our parasitical certainty by the guarantee of full employment.' And proceeds 'I think it is clear to everyone that we owe much of today's disorder, drunkenness and shoddy workmanship to over-employment' and adds 'a real danger of losing one's job and going on temporary unemployment pay or have to work where one is sent is rather good medicine against sloth, drunkenness and irresponsibility. Many experts felt that it should be cheaper to pay adequate unemployment compensation for a few months for such temporary unemployed than it is to keep a lot of loafers in the work force.'

Strangely, such apologists for capitalism ignore the reality of the capitalist world. Drunkenness and sloth are the product of unemployment and frustration and not that of over-employment.

By placing the burden of stagnation on the habits of the working class such ideologues have interpreted the CPSU's understanding of transforming the economy from socialist extensive to an intensive pattern, to mean the restoration of a capitalist labour market.

In the economic sphere, the equivalent of the bourgeois concept of 'absolute or pure democracy' is the objective 'laws of economic life'. Invoking the new economic policy and placing it as the only method of socialist economic construction, these academicians deliberately ignore what Lenin had to say about the NEP. Lenin in his report to the Second Congress of the Political Education Department, in early 1921, states 'the New Economic Policy needs substituting for the requisitioning of food; it means reverting to capitalism to a considerable extent – to what extent we do not know.' And states 'the issue in the present war is – who will win, who will first take advantage of the situation: the capitalist whom we are allowing to come in by the backdoor, and even by several doors (and by many doors we are not aware of and which open without us and despite us) or the proletarian state power?' And then Lenin poses the question, 'The whole question is – who will take the lead? We must face this issue squarely. Who will come out on the top? Either the capitalist succeeds in organizing first – in which case they will drive out the communists and that will be the end of it. Or, the proletarian state power with the support of the peasantry, will prove capable of keeping a proper rein on those gentlemen so as to direct capitalism along state channels and create a capitalism that will be subservient to the state and serve the same.'

The NEP was not only a economic measure, its political content was to cement, in those difficult years, the unity between the working class and the peasantry and to draw the peasantry into the process of socialist construction. Within a year the correctness of the policy produced the desired results and to the 11th Congress of the CPSU, in March 1922, Lenin states, 'For a year we have been retreating. In the name of the Party we must now call a halt. The purpose pursed by the retreat has been achieved. The period is drawing or has drawn to a close. Now our purpose is different – to regroup our forces.' In the subsequent period, the implementation of the five-year plans and collectivization laid the solid foundations for the socialist economy. Now six decades later and ironically, on the basis of the strength provided by these economic foundations, these academicians argue for the restoration of capitalist relations as the only means of correction of the 'command administer' type of economic management to overcome the recent relative stagnation.

Agrarian Reforms

At the 19th All-Union Conference of the CPSU, Gorbachev no longer talks in terms of 'consolidation of socialism' but of 'changing the relations of production'. Identifying the solving of the food problem as the key issue in improving the economy, Gorbachev argues for introducing private farms on a contractual long-term lease basis which will overcome the 'estrangement of labour'. Earlier in his book *Perestroika*, referring to the experience six decades of collectivization, Gorbachev states 'it is evident from the examples of collectives of contractual and family run farms how our people have missed the proprietary role'.

In a report to the CPSU Plenary meeting in March 1989 on the 'Agrarian Policy of the CPSU in the present conditions'

Gorbachev says, 'The point at issue here is the transfer of land and other means of production to the lease holders, their real control over these means, including the independent formation of the production structure and the contractual right of the lease holder to dispose of the lease based income and so on. It is important to make a new and, I would say, a decisive step and move from the establishment of individual lease holding collectives on a farm to having all the farm units operating on lease principles so that these principles embrace all the forms of inter-related production cycles.'

In other words, in the agrarian structure, in the name of overcoming the alienation of the farmer which is wrongly identified as the cause for declining rate of production, what is suggested is the dismantling of the collectives and reintroduction of the individual small scale, peasant economy.

This takes us back to the debates of the 1920s and even those currently raging in capitalist countries on the advocacy of peasant farming versus large-scale production in agriculture. While peasant farming may induce larger quantities of work input (even this is not absolutely necessary under all conditions) experience of both capitalist and socialist agriculture shows that large-scale organization of agriculture not only permits technological advance to be introduced and utilized, but provides the marketable surplus to feed the industrial work force. This latter factor is the key that sustained the process of industrialization both in the capitalist countries and the socialist Soviet Union. The rapid fructification of the five-year plans would have been impossible but for the food surplus turned out, as a result of the collectivization drive which sustained the growing industrial work force.

Such measures of re-introducing capitalist relations would actually lead to decline in the marketable surplus required to sustain the industrial work force.

In the sphere of agriculture, we see that the effect of such reforms was at dismantling of the socialist structure, instead of improving the efficiency in the collectives and cooperatives.

Ironically, in July 1990 Gorbachev himself had to state to the CPSU Central Committee, that the main problem on the food front 'lies in stopping losses while preserving harvests and livestock products and securing their high quality.' He adds, 'This is the shortest way to improving food supplies in the immediate future. Resolving this issue will enable us to increase food stocks by at least 15 to 20 per cent.'

An improvement of 15 to 20 per cent would have offset the current imports of food grains to the Soviet Union. Surely such improvements in economic management had not required a change in production relations of the nature suggested by Gorbachev! Hence, we see that in the name of overcoming the present-day difficulties of socialist production, capitalist prescriptions were being introduced that finally led to the dismantling of the socialist economic edifice.

Industry

In the sphere of industry and macro-economic planning relating to monetary and fiscal policy, a large number of decrees and laws were adopted over these years, whose essential basis was aimed at what the CPSU 28th Congress called, the 'transition to a full-fledged market economy'.

The purpose of all these, now it is clear, was to reduce if not dismantle, central planning, thus undermining the basic foundations of the socialist economy.

The law of enterprises promulgated in June 1987 gave the enterprises the power to independently deal with the other enterprises which was later amended to include trade with foreign firms and to set its own wages. The central plan authorities were required to reduce their quota of state orders to at least 70 per cent of the enterprises output, permitting the enterprises to privately and individually deal with the manner of the disposal of the rest of the 30 per cent.

Industrial production was thus no longer the result of a central plan based on the laws of balanced economic development and in correspondence with the peoples' requirement.

As a result, the independent relations that the enterprises could now enter into without reference to the central authorities, created a situation of anarchy both in relation to foreign trade and internal product mix. In the sphere of foreign trade, one can see a peculiar pattern in that, while the import of machinery increased by nearly 2.5 billion roubles between 1984 and 1988, the imports of consumer items were less by 1.5 billion roubles between 1985 and 1988. Authoritative statistics have shown that during Gorbachev's leadership, import of food grains and consumer items fell by the equivalent of 8.5 billion roubles. These patterns only reflect the anarchic trends that result from the dismantling of the planned economy which run counter not only to the overall welfare of the people, but to economic development itself.

Another consequence of having brought about such reforms was that the state was unable to firmly garner revenue for its own expenditure, which was earlier based on taxes on the enterprises recovered through the sale and distribution of the entire production in the economy. This led to a situation where the government had to increasingly resort to budgetary deficits. In 1985 the budget deficit was a modest 18 million roubles which rose to nearly 120 billion by 1989 or 14% of the Soviet Union's GNP.

This naturally created a situation where inflation began rising rapidly thus fuelling discontent of the people who were already subjected to shortages.

In other words, reforms that started to renew socialism by introducing capitalist prescriptions had dismantled the production and distribution structure that existed all these decades and in its place introduced anarchy that led to a steady deterioration in economic conditions.

These also brought severe strains in the economic relations between the Centre and the republics and economic interconnection between the republics themselves.

In 1990, three plans were proposed towards the transition to a market economy. The first, known as the Shatalin plan, envisaged the full-scale restoration of capitalist relations in all spheres of the Soviet economy in 500 days. While this was not acceptable to large sections of the Supreme Soviet, the Russian parliament, under Boris Yeltsin's leadership, however introduced and adopted this plan on 1 November 1990.

The second plan, proposed by economist Leonid Abalkin was rejected by Gorbachev himself, and the third, was Gorbachev's own plan prepared by economist Abel Aganbegyan which was a compromise between the two earlier mentioned plans. This was adopted by the Supreme Soviet on 19 October 1990.

The common thread, that runs through all these plans is the restoration of capitalist relations. The difference being only in the pace.

In the meanwhile, in May 1990, the Supreme Soviet completed a debate on the government's blueprint for the transition to a regulated market economy. This was a prelude for the adoption of the earlier mentioned plan in October. The government had decided on a course of freeing the prices of essential commodities and tripling the price of bread, which is the staple diet of the Soviet citizens. The plan was to ultimately free all prices to be fixed in relation to their demand in the market, thus abolishing for the first time in 70 years, the Soviet state's responsibility to ensure the right to live of every citizen.

By the end of 1991, the price of one kg of prime sausages which is avidly consumed by all Soviet citizens, equals the monthly pension of a retired officer!

Plan and Market

An issue that is of relevance to communists and socialists the world over is to understand the relation between the plan and the market.

Market exists as long as commodities are produced, as this is the economic sphere where commodities are exchanged. The question, therefore, is not whether market should exist under socialism. As long as commodities are produced, it exists. The moot question is which assumes the central role of economic activity, the plan or the market?

Market nowhere has ever existed or exists, even in the most developed capitalist countries, completely independent of the state. Even in the most advanced capitalist countries, the state controls the monetary and fiscal levers, which it manipulates to either advance or retard the basis of economic activity. So, the question once again is not the complete independence of the market from the state. It is the question of which controls the important economic levers – the declared priorities of the socialist state or that of the market.

The market, under capitalism, serves as the mechanism through which independent capitalists discern the rates of profit, which is the guiding force of the capitalist economic system. The market dynamics, in a sense, are the economic symbols which determine both the levels of production as well as the types of products that should be produced.

Under socialism, when the state guarantees such rights which are not guaranteed under bourgeois rule, the State's priorities in fulfilling these responsibilities assume precedence over the profitability indicators of the market. In the final analysis, it boils down to the question of who controls the state or whose class rule it is. Under bourgeois class rule, it is the profit indicators that are the driving force. Under working-class rule, it is the society's responsibilities that are the priorities.

However, it would be wrong to say that the market has no role to play at all under socialism. Being the economic sphere of commodity exchange, the demand and supply indicators permit the plan authorities to more effectively and rationally use resources. Instead, if market indicators are used to determine what should be produced and how much, depending on the free play of prices, then the social responsibility of the socialist state to provide the basic requirements of social welfare will have to be calculated on the market prices. This is precisely what Yeltsin and the Shatalin plan are bringing into operation in the Russian republic. The immediate consequence of this is that the social welfare rights will no longer be guaranteed, but will be available only to those who can afford them. The restoration of full-fledged market economy under socialism only means making production responsive to market indicators and that the decisions of what will be produced will be determined by profitability and not the social commitment to the people. Thus undermining, the very basis of the working class state.

There also arises under such reforms the question of who will appropriate the profit thus generated. These reforms, giving the right of profit appropriation to the concerned enterprises, have already led to wage disparities, are not commensurate with the work put in, and undermine the very basis of socialist production relations.

In the sphere of the economy, in all sectors – agriculture, industry, trade, fiscal and monetary policies and the market – the reforms brought under the guise of renewal of socialism actually paved the way for the restoration of capitalism. In the name of transition to market economy, what was done was to emphasize private initiative through personal profit and greed rather than socialist consciousness and solidarity as an instrument for stimulating production. Further, reliance was sought to be placed on small units in industry and agriculture (when purely in economic terms this was abandoned as less efficient by capitalist countries themselves) as the means to increase labour productivity rather than the application of science and technology to large-scale production.

IV

This triumph of counter-revolutionary forces in the Soviet Union and their undermining of the Great October Socialist Revolution have thrown up many theoretical questions regarding the political economy of socialism.

Marx's analysis was confined to what he said 'the laws of motion of modern society'. By modern society, he meant capitalism. A lot of work still remains to be done for the study of the political economy of other modes of production. The existence and experience of socialism has demonstrated that a lot more has to be done with regard to the political economy of socialism.

Engels, in *Anti-Duhring*, defines political economy in the following manner,

> Political economy is the science of the laws governing the production and exchange of material means of subsistence in human society. The conditions under which men produce and exchange vary from country to country and within one country from generation to generation. Political economy, therefore, cannot be the same for all countries or for all historical epochs . . . Political economy, therefore, is essentially a historical science. It deals with material that is historical that is constantly changing . . . at the same time it goes without saying that the

> laws that are valid for a definite mode of production and of exchange hold good for all historical periods in which these modes of production and forms of exchange prevail.

Engels was thus clearly warning, that while the fundamental laws of political economy remain valid for the entire period of the mode of production, as productive forces develop within this mode of production itself constantly changing the conditions under which production takes places, the economic and therefore social relations also change. A proper detailed study of the political economy of socialism unfortunately was lagging.

This has been clearly so during the last four decades particularly since after Stalin's *Economic Problems of Socialism in the USSR*. There, he had stated 'relying on the economic law that the relations of production must necessarily conform with the character of the productive forces, the Soviet government socialized the means of production, made them property of the whole people and thereby abolished the exploiting system and created the socialist forms of economy. Had it not been for this law and had the Soviet Government not relied upon it, it could not have accomplished this mission.' He proceeds to state 'one of the distinguishing features of political economy is, that its laws, unlike those of natural science are impermanent. They, or at least a majority of them, operate for a definite historical period after which they give place to new laws, which are not created by the will of man but which arise from new economic conditions.'

While correctly identifying the stagnation that set in the Soviet economy in the seventies, as due to the non-correspondence of the methods of economic management to the developing social productive forces, the Gorbachev leadership had, instead of drawing from the experience of economic construction under the socialized means of production, advocated capitalist reforms as the cure to socialism's problems of growth. The international bourgeoisie, which never did reconcile itself to the establishment and development of socialism, found ideal circumstances to intervene and strengthen the internal forces of counter-revolution for the dismantling of socialism.

These developments have also brought to the fore the necessity to carry out a deeper analysis, which, as the CPI(M)'s Draft Resolution *On Ideological Issues* states, 'has been hindered . . . by revisionism and dogmatism in the communist movement which, in turn, led to theoretical stagnation to a certain extent.' This is a task that needs to be carried forward in order to correctly absorb the experience of building socialism in the Soviet Union and strengthening of future struggles for socialism.

PART III

THE PRESENT

You who live in this Sour Little Age cannot imagine the grandeur of the prospect we gazed upon: like standing atop the highest peak in the mighty Caucasus, and viewing in one all-knowing glance the mountainous, granite order of creation. You cannot imagine it. I weep for you.

And what have you to offer now, children of this Theory? What have you to offer in its place? Market Incentives? American Cheeseburgers? Watered-down Bukharinite stopgap makeshift Capitalism! NEPmen! Pygmy children of a gigantic race!

Change? Yes, we must change, only show me the Theory, and I will be at the barricades, show me the book of the next Beautiful Theory, and I promise you these blind eyes will see again, just to read it, to devour that text. Show me the words that will reorder the world, or else keep silent.

If the snake sheds his skin before a new skin is ready, naked he will be in the world, prey to the forces of chaos. Without his skin he will be dismantled, lose coherence and die. Have you, my little serpents, a new skin?

Tony Kushner, *Perestroika*, 1995

GLOBALIZATION AND THE IMPASSE OF CAPITALISM

Prabhat Patnaik

I feel greatly honoured that I have been asked to deliver the Harold Wolpe memorial lecture for the year 2016. Harold Wolpe was an outstanding thinker who combined political activism for the liberation of the South African people with deep insights into the economic basis of apartheid. I am indeed grateful for this opportunity to pay my tribute to this remarkable person who in my view constitutes a role model for anyone aspiring to be a social scientist. Since a good deal of Harold Wolpe's theoretical work was concerned with the value of labour power, and hence by implication with income distribution, I thought it would not be inapposite if I use this opportunity to say something on income distribution in the world economy in the current era of globalization.

Many authors have seen the current episode of globalization not as an altogether novel phenomenon, but only as a continuation, after a certain period of interruption, of earlier episodes of globalization. There is some truth in this perception, since capitalism from the very beginning has been a global phenomenon that has forced open, and incorporated into its own orbit, economies from all over the globe. It has never been what 'mainstream' economics typically portrays it to be, namely a 'closed system' consisting exclusively of capitalists and workers, and developing largely on its own resources, and at best engaging in peaceful international trade at the margin to the mutual benefit of all trading parties.

There is however a fundamental difference between the current episode of globalization and all previous episodes, and this consists in the fact that the current episode is characterized by a mobility not just of capital-as-finance across the globe but also of capital-in-production. And the latter occurs in order to take advantage of the low real wages prevailing in the third world economies to locate activities there, not so much for meeting local demand as for meeting global demand.

This had never happened before, for if it had then the division of the world into an advanced and a backward segment would not have occurred. This division arose because while the encroachment of metropolitan capital into third world economies through colonial or semi-colonial domination had created massive labour reserves in the latter by destroying the basis of local petty production, there had been little absorption of such reserves into modern capitalist production. This was because capitalist production had developed only to a limited extent in these economies *owing to the reluctance of metropolitan capital to locate production there to take advantage of the lower wages*. The only activities that drew metropolitan capital into the third world were mining and plantations, and the complementary spheres of trade and finance to service such primary commodity specialization, but not manufacturing activities for meeting the global market. The third world economies therefore remained mired in mass poverty which was generated by this specific form of their integration into the orbit of world capitalism.

The export of capital that did occur on a large scale from the capitalist metropolis was into the temperate regions of European settlement like Canada, Australia, New Zealand and the United States, where capital exports went together with labour emigration. European migration into these temperate regions ousted the local inhabitants from their lands, and even virtually decimated them, so that the immigrants who took over these lands enjoyed a high income. This high income ensured a high 'reservation wage' for workers both in the countries they came to and also in the countries they came from. (South Africa too was a destination for European migrants but in its case the local inhabitants were not decimated as elsewhere but became instead a subjugated low-wage work-force).

This high reservation wage, indeed the higher reservation wage in the metropolitan countries compared to the third world economies, has been attributed by writers like W. Arthur Lewis to the fact that England and other European countries had higher land and labour productivity (assuming identical land-labour ratios everywhere) than third world countries like India and China, because of the agricultural revolution that is supposed to have occurred in the former.[1] This view however is untenable. There is little evidence of any agricultural revolution occurring in England or elsewhere;[2] on the other hand the fact of European immigrants ousting the original inhabitants in the temperate regions, shepherding those of them who managed to survive into 'reservations', and setting themselves up as farmers with a high per capita income because of the favourable land-man ratio, and thereby ensuring a high reservation wage both in Europe and in the 'new world', is quite indubitable.

The scale of migration was extremely large. Lewis estimates that fifty million Europeans migrated to the temperate regions of the 'new world' in the nineteenth century, while an equal number of Chinese and Indian workers migrated as 'coolie' or 'indentured' labour to the tropical regions of the world at the behest of metropolitan capital. These two streams were kept separate: one was a low-wage migration (not surprising in view of the massive unemployment created through the destruction of local petty production in tropical colonies and semi-colonies) and the other was a high-wage migration (for reasons already discussed).

These absolute numbers mentioned by Lewis do not give a

[1] W. A. Lewis, *The Evolution of the International Economic* Order, Princeton: Princeton University Press, 1978.

[2] Utsa Patnaik, 'The Agricultural Revolution in England: Its Cost for the English Working Class and the Colonies', in Shireen Moosvi ed. *Capitalism, Colonialism and Globalization*, Delhi: Tulika Books, 2011.

proper idea of the scale of migration. A better idea is obtained by comparing emigration with the population of the home country in question. Thus from Great Britain which had a population of 14 million in 1815 there was an emigration of 16 million persons between 1815 and 1910; in fact roughly half of the gross addition to the British population each year in this period emigrated to the 'new world'.[3] And along with the migration of labour there was as Brinley Thomas has shown a complementary migration of capital, which brought about an immense diffusion of capitalism from Europe to the 'new world' (but not to the third world).

The colonial and semi-colonial economies of the third world were made to aid this diffusion, from which they themselves were excluded, in at least two ways.[4] One was through their being yoked to a triangular pattern of trade. British goods like textiles for instance were not demanded in the 'new world', so that capital exports from Britain, which was the largest capital exporter in the period up to the first world war, *could not take the commodity-form of British-produced goods*. These goods therefore were sold in markets like India and China; and primary commodities produced by these economies, which *were* demanded by the 'new world', were exported by Britain as the commodity-form of its own capital exports.

The second way was through the extraction of a surplus by the use of the taxation-system from colonies like India, which was expropriated by Britain without any *quid pro quo* and which financed British capital exports. An economy like

[3] These figures are taken from Utsa Patnaik, 'Capitalism and the Production of Poverty', *Social Scientist,* Vol.40, Numbers 1 and 2, January-February 2012.

[4] The discussion in this paragraph and the one that follows is based on Prabhat Patnaik and Utsa Patnaik, *A Theory of Imperialism*, New York: Columbia University Press, 2016.

India for instance was not only made to absorb British goods, unwanted in the 'new world', at the expense of its own 'de-industrialization' resulting in the displacement of its artisans and craftsmen, but was in addition made to export more goods than it imported, with the export surplus being credited not as its own capital exports but as that of Britain. India's current account of the balance of payments was made to appear as balanced, thereby denying it any credit for its export surplus, through a whole range of fictitious service import items, which amounted in effect to payments by India for the privilege of being governed by the colonial master. These fictitious service import items were used to offset its export surplus. Despite having the second largest export surplus in the period 1900-1928, second only to the United States, India over this very period did not accumulate a single penny of net claims on other economies; on the contrary it even got marginally into debt with Britain.

What concerns me here however is the manner in which this entire arrangement overcame the aggregate demand problem of metropolitan capitalism. There were three elements involved here. First, there was the diffusion of capitalism, or the pushing of the 'frontier', which provided the basic stimulus to the system. Second, this stimulus could be utilized only because of the fact that the colonial markets were 'on tap',[5] so that home produced commodities within the metropolis could be converted into commodities demanded in the 'new world' via the colonial markets. Or, if one wishes to decompose the demand problem by drawing a distinction between the problem of aggregate demand and the problem of 'disproportionality', then one can say that the former was resolved by the expanding frontier and the latter by colonial

[5] This expression is used by S. B. Saul, *Studies in British Overseas Trade*, Liverpool: Liverpool University Press, 1960.

trade. And third, the tightness in the metropolitan labour market produced by mass emigration also meant that real wages could rise alongside labour productivity, which also made the problem of aggregate demand more tractable.[6] If such a wage increase had not happened, then a rise in labour productivity in the face of constant or near-constant real wages would have meant an increase in the share of surplus in the output of the metropolis, which, as Baran and Sweezy, relying on the work of Kalecki, have shown, produces a tendency towards over-production because of the higher 'propensity to consume' of the wage-earners compared to the surplus earners.[7] This was kept at bay because of the segmentation of the world economy, which made it possible for metropolitan wages to rise with labour productivity, even as third world wages stagnated at some subsistence level owing to the existence of large third world labour reserves. This divergence in real wage movement could be sustained, because neither did metropolitan capital flow into the third world nor was third world labour allowed to flow into the metropolis.

The earlier episode of globalization in short was of a kind that, by its very nature of being wrapped within a colonial system, involving both the 'colonies of settlement' (the 'new world') and the 'colonies of conquest' (in the third world), did not face a problem of aggregate demand. This is the reason that metropolitan capitalism experienced the prolonged boom of the Victorian and the Edwardian era, or the 'Long Boom of the Long Twentieth Century'. The collapse of this boom after the first world war can be attributed to the collapse of the conditions which had sustained it. Of these, three in

[6] Joan Robinson, 'Introduction' to Rosa Luxemburg's *Accumulation of Capital*, London, Routledge, 1963.

[7] Paul Baran and Paul Sweezy, *Monopoly Capital*, New York: Monthly Review Press, 1966 and M. Kalecki, *The Theory of Economic Dynamics*, London: Allen and Unwin, 1954.

particular deserve mention: the 'closing of the frontier' which Alvin Hansen was to emphasize; the encroachment of Japan into the Asian markets of Britain which made the triangular pattern of settlement unsustainable; and the world agricultural crisis which reduced primary commodity prices and had the same effect, of making the triangular pattern of settlement untenable.

The Great Depression of the 1930s occurred precisely because metropolitan capitalism in that period did not have any such arrangement in place to overcome its problem of aggregate demand: the old colonial arrangement had ceased to work (in any case, as Rosa Luxemburg had argued, it could provide only a transitory stimulus), and no new arrangement had been created to take its place. Such a new arrangement came into being only in the post-second world war period with the introduction of Keynesian-style State intervention in demand management in each metropolitan country, and above all in the United States, within the overarching framework of the Bretton Woods system. This ushered in what has been called a 'Golden Age of capitalism'. *And the point to note about the current episode of globalization is that it entails an end of that arrangement, and hence of the 'Golden Age'.*

State intervention in demand management necessarily entails intervention by the *nation-State,* and if the nation-State is to have the autonomy to intervene successfully, then finance itself must be 'national', and not globalized. Keynes had been well aware of this and had argued explicitly in an article in *The Yale Review* of 1933 that finance must be national; and under the Bretton Woods system, of which he was one of the architects, countries could, and did, impose capital controls to ensure that finance did remain national, so that the nation-State had the autonomy to undertake demand management.[8]

[8] J. M. Keynes, 'National Self-Sufficiency', *The Yale Review*, Vol. 22, no.

The current episode of globalization whose main hallmark is the globalization of capital, including above all of finance capital, has ended this. The autonomy of the nation-State is undermined, since the State has to be careful not to upset the 'confidence of the investors' (a euphemism for international finance capital), for otherwise in the new situation where there is unconstrained cross-border capital movements, finance would flow out of the country precipitating a financial crisis. State policy therefore gets determined in accordance with the demands of international finance capital. Since finance capital favours both reduced taxes on the rich (for obvious reasons) and 'sound finance', i.e. keeping the fiscal deficit restricted to a certain small proportion of the gross domestic product (usually three percent these days and not zero as in the days of the Gold Standard), the State's ability to undertake demand management gets undermined. It can neither run a large enough fiscal deficit, nor rely on the 'balanced budget multiplier' to lift the economy out of a state of stagnation or recession. The State's ability to increase welfare expenditure is also restricted in such a regime of globalized finance for the same reasons, but I am concerned here only with the issue of aggregate demand.

The question that will be raised immediately against this argument, that globalization brings in its train a problem of deficiency of aggregate demand, is the following: even if what is discussed above may be true of other countries from which capital may flow out if the nation-State does not strictly follow the dictates of finance, can it also be true of the United States whose currency is considered to be 'as good as gold' by the world's wealth-holders, and which therefore cannot possibly experience any capital flight? Why should the US not continue then to follow policies of demand management as

....

4, June 1933.

before, which could also raise the level of activity of the world economy as a whole?

There is an obvious answer to this question. Any action by the US State to boost demand, say through an enlarged fiscal deficit, will necessarily entail the leaking out of a part of this demand in the form of imports from other countries. In the absence of greater protectionism in the US, any attempt by its State to stimulate domestic activity will necessarily therefore entail an increase in its external indebtedness, and that too for generating employment in other countries, like China. Since the US State continues after all to be a nation-State, it can scarcely be expected to get into debt for generating employment elsewhere. This is why within the current regime of globalization, i.e. in the absence of US protectionism, even the country that should not fear any capital flight if it pursued an expansionary policy, is reluctant to do so.

A deeper question would also be asked of the above argument. And that is: why should finance capital insist on 'sound finance' when the effect of such 'sound finance' is to prolong a state of recession and stagnation, which discredits, and hence threatens, the system as a whole? This demand of finance for balancing budgets is not new; it has always been there. It was there even in 1929 when the British Treasury, under the influence of the City of London, had turned down Lloyd George's proposal, made on Keynes' suggestion, to start a public works programme, financed by a fiscal deficit, to take care of the growing unemployment which had already reached 10 per cent by that date.[9] Why should there be this demand at all?

The answer to this question, of why finance capital is opposed to fiscal deficits, goes beyond narrow economic considerations, such as the fear of inflation or the fear of

[9] Joan Robinson, *Economic Philosophy*, London: C. A. Watts, 1962.

an exchange rate depreciation which finance may entertain in the event of a stimulation of activity. Such fears may conceivably arise near the top of a boom, but not in the midst of a recession; and while such fears may be legitimate in the case of some countries, they cannot possibly explain the *universal* opposition of finance to fiscal deficits, an opposition described by Joan Robinson as 'the humbug of finance'.[10] This opposition, I believe, springs rather from a fear of the system's losing its social legitimacy. If State intervention, bypassing the route of boosting the 'animal spirits' of capitalists through providing 'incentives' to them, becomes the established procedure for expanding the level of activity, then the question will inevitably be raised: why do we need the capitalists at all, why not have State control over production? Keynesian-style State intervention in demand management in other words constitutes a violation of the standard 'rules of the game' of the system; and even though, in the aftermath of the second world war, finance capital may have acquiesced in such a violation, when its very existence was under threat, it re-establishes these rules whenever it gets an opportunity to do so, such as what globalization of finance in a world of nation-States has provided.

There is a second way in which the current globalization generates a serious problem of deficiency of aggregate demand.[11] Its hallmark, we have seen, is to overcome the earlier segmentation of the world economy, which means that the real wages in the advanced capitalist economies are no longer immune to the baneful consequences of third world labour reserves. As long as these reserves last, not only do

[10] See also Prabhat Patnaik, 'The Humbug of Finance', *The Retreat to Unfreedom*, Delhi: Tulika Books, 2002.

[11] Prabhat Patnaik, 'A Marxist Perspective on the World Economy', *Marx's Capital: An Introductory Reader*, New Delhi: LeftWord Books, 2011.

third world wages remain tied to a subsistence level, but even metropolitan wages, while they do not exactly come down to equal third world wages, cease to increase as before because of competition from cheap third world labour. Even though labour is still not free to move from the third to the first world, since capital is now willing to move from the first to the third world to take advantage of the wage-differential, this very fact restricts wage increases in the first world.

The vector of world real wages therefore does not increase even as labour productivity increases everywhere, causing an increase in the share of surplus in world output. In the United States for instance between 1968 and 2011 according to Joseph Stiglitz the absolute level of the real wage of a male worker has not increased (if anything it has decreased marginally), even though there has obviously been a massive increase in labour productivity over this long period.

A rise in the share of surplus in total output has the effect *ceteris paribus* of reducing aggregate demand, as mentioned earlier, for a simple reason highlighted by authors like Kalecki, Steindl, and Baran and Sweezy, namely that the consumption-income ratio is higher for wage-earners than for surplus earners.[12] Such a shift therefore has the effect of reducing aggregate consumption, and hence aggregate demand for any given level of investment. Since the actual investment in any period is based on investment decisions taken in the past, and hence is more or less given, such a shift therefore tends *actually* to reduce the level of aggregate demand and hence output, which in turn lowers investment in the next period, causing a cumulative tendency towards stagnation. Such a tendency becomes even more pronounced when the increase in the share of surplus is not once-for-all but continuous.

[12] Kalecki, *The Theory of Economic Dynamics*; Baran & Sweezy, *Monopoly Capitalism*; J. Steindl, *Maturity and Stagnation in American Capitalism*, New York: Monthly Review Press, 1976.

It follows therefore that the current globalization, apart from preventing State intervention in demand management and hence giving rise to a problem of aggregate demand for that reason, also tends to reduce aggregate demand by raising the share of surplus in world output.

One aspect of this increase in the share of surplus in world output, *which manifests itself within every country,* since labour productivity rises everywhere even as real wages remain stagnant everywhere, has received much attention; and that relates to the growing inequality in income and wealth across the globe. Of course the rise in inequality has not been analyzed along the lines outlined above by those like Thomas Piketty who have written about it. They have used other explanations, such as for instance (in Piketty's case) the fact that the rate of profit has exceeded the rate of population growth. But in general such theoretical explanations have been either logically or empirically untenable, which is also true of Piketty's own explanation.[13] A more persuasive explanation of the observed increase in income and wealth inequality within each country in the world lies in the fact that globalization has kept down wages everywhere even as labour productivity has gone up everywhere.

Some have argued that since economies like China and India have grown rapidly during this era of globalization, even though inequalities may have increased within them, there has been a reduction in inequalities across the *countries of the world.* But, because of the significant increase in inequalities within these countries, if we take say rural and urban China as two separate countries and likewise rural and urban India, then we are likely to find that inequalities, as measured for instance by the Gini coefficient, across the countries of the

[13] Prabhat Patnaik, 'Capitalism, Inequality and Globalization: A Review of Thomas Piketty', *MRZine*, 17 October 2014.

world so defined, have also increased. This is what one would expect since the bulk of the labour reserves in the world are located in the rural areas of these vast economies. The point I wish to make however is that while the social and political significance of the increase in inequality, such as its effect in enfeebling democracy, has received attention, its economic effect in terms of causing stagnation and recession through a reduction in aggregate demand has hardly been recognized. (In Piketty's analysis the problem of aggregate demand does not even enter, since it is based on neo-classical growth theory which assumes Say's Law that supply creates its own demand).

Of course if the growth process in the era of globalization could significantly exhaust the labour reserves then this increase in inequality, and with it the tendency towards stagnation, should disappear. But paradoxically the fact of growing inequality itself produces a growth process whereby the labour reserves, far from disappearing, tend to increase in relative size. To see why this is so, let us for a moment forget about the tendency towards stagnation that growing inequality produces (this tendency would strengthen the argument presented below) and assume that the consumption-income ratios of the wage earners and the surplus earners are equal.

Now a dollar shifted from the poor to the rich, even if it generates the same consumption expenditure, entails expenditure on very different sets of commodities. Typically expenditure by the rich is on goods and services which are much less employment-intensive than those which the working people demand. This is because technological progress under capitalism in the form of process and product innovations has the character generally of economizing on labour (which after all is why labour productivity increases over time), and the rich demand more up-to-date goods than the poor. A rise in the share of surplus therefore, which entails a shift in income distribution from the working poor to the rich, raises the time-profile of productivity along any particular growth path. But if there is a continuous increase in the share of surplus, then for any given rate of growth of output the time-profile of labour productivity itself keeps increasing from one period to the next, i.e. the observed rate of growth of labour productivity itself keeps increasing over time. Since the rate of growth of employment is merely the difference between the rate of growth of output and the rate of growth of labour productivity, this implies that for any given rate of growth of output, employment growth keeps slowing down over time. With any given rate of growth of the work-force therefore if employment growth, to start with is not such as to prevent a rise in the share of surplus, *it will never do so over time and the relative labour reserves will eventually keep increasing in size.*

It follows therefore that no matter what the rate of growth of output, if it does not prevent an increase in the share of surplus at all, then it necessarily tends eventually to enlarge the relative size of the labour reserves for any given rate of growth of the work-force. The share of surplus in such a case keeps increasing, and the growth process leads not just to a perpetuation of the existing size of the labour reserves relative to the work-force but to an increasing relative size of such reserves.

I have so far assumed a given rate of growth of output. In fact however, as we have seen, even the maintenance of this growth becomes impossible owing to the tendency towards over-production arising from the rise in the share of surplus. It follows therefore that the third world labour reserves never get exhausted if the share of surplus rises over time; on the contrary the relative size of labour reserves increases despite the fact that capital-in-production in the current era of globalization moves to third world economies from the metropolitan centres to meet global demand.

This phenomenon is further compounded by another factor. The tendency under capitalism is to destroy pre-capitalist petty production. But in the post-second world war years of *dirigiste* development in the third world, the governments that came to power in the newly-liberated countries tended to protect petty producers from going under, in part-fulfilment of the promises made during the anti-colonial struggle. With the end of *dirigisme* and the introduction of neo-liberal policies, the spontaneous tendency of capitalism to destroy petty production reasserts itself, as the State, under compulsion to accede to the demands of globalized finance for maintaining its 'confidence', ceases to provide petty producers with the support and protection needed for their viability. The petty producers displaced in this manner from their traditional occupations seek employment outside, which adds to the supply of the job-seeking work-force in the capitalist sector. But with meagre employment generation in the capitalist sector, these displaced petty producers only add to the relative size of the labour reserves.

Hence the proposition that the current regime of globalization is associated with a tendency towards stagnation remains unimpaired. Or, putting it differently, the current episode of globalization which entails a newfound mobility of capital to take advantage of the low third world wages and which therefore is presented as an achievement of capitalism, is actually the harbinger of a structural crisis, an impasse for capitalism. This impasse may get camouflaged, and indeed did get camouflaged for some time, by the formation of 'bubbles' in asset prices, first the dot-com bubble and later the housing bubble, which have the capacity to boost aggregate demand. 'Bubbles' in short constitute the one possible antidote to the structural crisis, but with their inevitable bursting the crisis gets exposed. And since new bubbles cannot be made to order, the crisis that their bursting creates may continue for a protracted period of time, as we are seeing today.

The crisis following the bursting of the housing 'bubble' which began in 2007-08 continues unabated to this day in the advanced capitalist world, and is even spreading to the erstwhile fast-growing economies like India and China. The point I am trying to make in short is that the current phase of capitalism witnesses not just transient crises of the familiar kind, but something fundamentally different, which is in fact a veritable impasse for capitalism. It is comparable to the 1930s crisis but even more serious in the sense that there are no ideas whatsoever on how it can be overcome.

This impasse has brought great distress to the working people all over the world. In the advanced capitalist countries not only have real wages stagnated, as we have seen, but employment too has declined with the unleashing of the protracted crisis. In the third world economies, the destruction of petty production, which constitutes a process of 'primitive accumulation of capital', the absence of employment growth and the consequent increase in the size of the relative labour reserves, and the stagnation of real wages of even the employed workers that has followed, combine to cause acute distress among the working people.

Alleviating this distress requires intervention by the State. But in the absence of a World State, or even the prospects of one, which could effect Keynesian-style demand management at the world level, even against the wishes of globalized finance capital, the only possibility that remains is for the nation-State to undertake a similar intervention by delinking the national economy from globalization. This would require however a change in the class character of the State, since it would entail confronting international finance capital.

The Left that should be leading the struggle for such a

change, appears everywhere unfortunately to believe that the current globalization, dominated by international finance capital, can simply be carried forward to a higher form of globalization that has shaken off this domination, *without any transitional delinking by any national economy*. Despite its criticism of current globalization therefore it sees any delinking from it as reactionary, while at the same time lacking any alternative agenda for improving the conditions of the working people. This has left the way open for a growth of fascist forces who explain the distress of the people not as the working of the system that has culminated in the current globalization but by invoking an evil 'other': the immigrant, the Muslim, or the foreign worker who 'steals jobs'.

These forces are opposed not to the globalization of capital but to immigration (and, possibly, to the unrestricted imports of foreign goods). The Left's endorsement even of the current globalization has the unfortunate effect therefore of making growing numbers of working people repose their faith in these racist and fascist forces. A polarization is thus being produced where the Left and the Liberals are on the same side as international finance capital, as proponents of globalization, but with no agenda for improving the people's condition, while the Right appears to offer an agenda , though it is only a racist or a fascist agenda.

This dichotomy is unfortunate. In cases, such as Bernie Sanders, where the Left has presented itself as being against the hegemony of international finance capital and the globalization dominated by it, it has struck a chord with the working people and posed a challenge to the fascist forces. But much of the Left seems as yet not to have grasped the need for delinking from globalization, because it has not grasped the impasse that capitalism has run into. It is for this reason that I have devoted the current lecture to this issue. Thank you.

THE PARTY AND THE COMMUNIST HORIZON

Jodi Dean

The United States of America needs a party – a militant, internationalist organization of the Left. Against Left realists who claim that the party is an outmoded or 'fully saturated' political form, that we are relegated to momentary acts of resistance or small reforms that leave the capitalist system intact, I argue that our conditions push us to rethink and renew that form of political organization through which communists think collectively about political power, act together in order to generate it, and inspire one another to use it for the collective determination of the world we produce in common. Capitalism pushes us apart. Left politics should not do the same. Instead of emphasizing difference, it should assert and build commonality. The party is a form for this assertion.

Over the last thirty odd years (at least since 1989), a 'Left realism' has taken hold of a certain northern, western, US-European left. At the site of a re-thought humanist, culturalist, post-structuralist post-Marxism is the foreclosure of revolution and the reduction of politics to critique, resignification, subversion, reform, resistance, and work on the self. Underlying continued aspirations for equality, real opposition to imperialism, racism, sexism, and homophobia, is the sense that our working class is privileged, included, and complacent. Radical politics involves other places, other subjects. Thus, during the same period that neoliberalism consolidated itself as a political-economic formation (or, in Foucault's terms, a 'governmentality'), most activists and intellectuals associated with the Left rejected not just specific communist parties but the very idea of the party as a form for radical political action.[1]

[1] On neoliberal governmentality, see Michel Foucault, *The Birth of*

Although some of the rejections repeat arguments against centralism found already in the split between Bolsheviks and Mensheviks or part of a councilist or ultra-left political current, others situate themselves in a line of criticism prominent in the late sixties and early seventies. Rightly frustrated with a system the components of which buttress rather than undermine capitalism, various voices on the Left began to amplify one another as they targeted their critical energies on the mediating institutions of capitalist society – family, union, party, and university. Insofar as these institutions made capitalism possible, that is, secured for it an adequate workforce and compliant citizenry, their abolition made seeming sense as a revolutionary goal. The party is but one of the institutions through which political energies are co-opted into the maintenance of the status quo – a critique levelled at the Communist Party USA during the years of the Popular Front as well as the French Communist Party in 1968, to give but two examples.

Now in the second decade of the new millennium, the mediating institutions of civil society have changed significantly. More people live alone than in any time in US history.[2] Fewer US children live in two-parent families.[3] Because of decades of anti-sexist and anti-homophobic struggle, even the mainstream accepts a wider array of living arrangements than were permitted thirty years ago. Union membership in the US is at its lowest level in a century.[4] Wages

....

Biopolitics, translated by Graham Burchell, New York: Palgrave Macmillan, 2008. For an example of rejection of the party, see Michael Hardt and Antonio Negri, *Empire*, Cambridge, MA: Harvard University Press, 2000.

2 Tim Henderson, 'More Americans living alone, census says,' the *Washington Post*, Sept. 28, 2014.

3 Gretchen Livingston, 'Less than half of U.S. kids today live in a 'traditional' family,' Pew Research Center, December 22, 2014.

4 Steven Greenhouse, 'Share of the Work Force in a Union Falls to a 97-

have correspondingly stagnated and declined, decreasing the likelihood that blue collar, service sector, and minimum wage jobs can lead to a middle class standard of living. Left political parties have either collapsed or compromized. Max Elbaum's account of the new communist movement of the seventies tells this story particularly well as it documents the setbacks facing US party-builders at the time, their inability to regroup in the eighties, and the broadly demobilizing effects of the end of state socialism on activists who had been 'anchors of popular movements'.[5] The situation of the university is less easy to summarize although it is clear, first, that as political commitment to public education – education as a recognized social good – has declined, student debt has soared, and, second, that education is a key front in today's class war.

Our current conjuncture differs from that of the sixties and early seventies in that individuals are now more likely to encounter state and market directly, without the protections of mediating institutions. Instead of what liberalism renders as the force *of* law, individuals encounter force *as* law, whether directly as police or indirectly as market. Communicative capitalist ideology presents this immediacy as direct conversations between individual and company, as entrepreneurialism, as flexible contract-based work. It mystifies it as personal responsibility, choice, DIY, 'pro-sumption' (the producer as consumer), and opportunity for creative input.[6] Privatization, off-shoring, precarity, and the decline of unions have contributed to the loss of working class jobs capable of sustaining a middle class quality of life. An effect has been the dismantling of the wide array of associations formerly part of working class culture. Not only is the working class not a

....

Year Low, 11.3%,' the *New York Times*, Jan. 23, 2013.

[5] Max Elbaum, *Revolution in the Air*, London: Verso, 2002, p. 293.

[6] For a discussion of communicative capitalist ideology see Jodi Dean, *Publicity's Secret*, Ithaca: Cornell University Press, 2002.

revolutionary class, but in the US it is barely conscious of itself as a class, a result, paradoxically, of the success of organized labour in fighting for collective bargaining and higher wages.

US culture is no longer mass culture. From personalized networked media, to eight hundred channel cable television, to the proliferation of sub- and micro-cultural consumption opportunities in the 'long tail' of music, video, and writing available on the internet, communicative capitalist culture offers multiple, innumerable, possibilities for expression, increasingly few of which register to any significant degree.[7] Our politics is likewise no longer mass politics. Mainstream electoral politics focuses so exclusively on fund-raising that the more poor people support a policy the less likely their representatives are to support it.[8] Left politics has also shed the mass dimension of the twentieth century. Configured through contemporary capitalism's push to customize, specify, and individuate, Left issue and identity politics reduces action to raising awareness in the hope of generating an emotional response intense enough to inspire people to find out more for themselves, get involved, and make their opinions known. The Left has mimicked and repeated in our politics the fragmentation, localization, and pluralization crucial to neoliberalism's dismantling of the welfare state. Even as capital has consolidated its class power and pursued a long-term strategy hostile to the rest of us, the Left accepts and augments its dispersion into singularized individuals. The few categories that make belonging explicit attempt at the same time to disavow collectivity: the consumer over the producers, the tax-payer over the public.

Commenting on a text he wrote in the mid-eighties with

[7] See Jodi Dean, *Democracy and Other Neoliberal Fantasies*, Durham: Duke University Press, 2009.

[8] Jacob S. Hacker and Paul Pierson, *Winner-Take-All-Politics*, New York: Simon and Schuster, 2011, p. 111.

Felix Guattari, Antonio Negri notes that the new organization of capitalist production in the late seventies produced a subjectivity 'locked in an insuperable contradiction, for social cooperation was more and more violently in opposition to the structures of capitalist control'.[9] He observes as well that even as he and Guattari recognized the importance of new technologies in networked communication, they didn't push their analysis far enough and that they should have detected new possibilities for rebellion. I would add that they should have identified new forms of capture and subjection.[10] Social media resolves and displaces the contradiction between social cooperation and capitalist control. Interacting through personalized, ubiquitous media we leave traces that can be archived and searched, sold to advertizers and turned over to security forces. We can connect with others, share our hopes and dreams, and reinforce capitalist control with the same clicks and links, likes and shares. We can be networked revolutionaries, courageously forwarding videos to all our friends. We can work on demand from home. Our mediated sociality affirms the structures of capitalist control more deeply and completely than the institutions of civil society ever did – especially under circumstances that amplify injunctions to individuality.

More than the mythic 'rugged individualism' of American frontier ideology, 'individuality' is an economic element of communicative capitalism. Getting a job, a contract, an opportunity requires that one demonstrate that one is *uniquely* qualified in what one knows to be a dense and competitive field.[11] As the market for middle class jobs contracts, one has

[9] Felix Guattari and Antonio Negri, *New Lines of Alliance, New Spaces of Liberty*, New York: Autonomedia, 2010, p. 104.

[10] See Mark Andrejevic, *iSpy*, Kansas City, Kansas: University Press of Kansas, 2007.

[11] See Carrie M. Lane, *A Company of One*, Ithaca: ILR Press, 2011.

to stand out from the pack, show that one is both a team player and capable of thinking outside the box, creative yet 'one of us'. The entrepreneurial relation to self (as well as to others that we see in the idea of 'social entrepreneurs') enhances the likelihood of education-related debt as well as credit card debt accrued in the interest of looking the part, projecting the appearance of success, and supporting work done for free (internships, volunteering). Capitalism's contradictions are interiorized in the form of the unique individual who is one of a multitude of singularities.

Mainstream culture describes the structural effects of the amplified competition underlying the injunction to uniqueness as the 'winner-take-all' or winner-take-most character of the new economy, the 80/20 rule, or (inversely) 'the long tail'. The basic idea is that any system characterized by free choice and preferential attachment will generate extreme inequality. Moreover, the larger the system, the larger the inequality. The stimulation of the production of uniqueness, of individualities, produces the field in which the individual dissolves so that a 'one', a winner, can emerge to claim the prize or get the job.[12] And even as there is a long tail, that is, a vast majority of losers (those who are much closer to each other that they are to the one), communicative capitalism produces these losers not as a mass but as a multitude of singularities, each holding on to its difference as its most valuable attribute despite its fundamental devaluation with respect to the system.

The genius of the slogan 'We are the 99%' is that it grasps this basic fact, names it, and occupies it. It recognizes the winner-take-all character of contemporary capitalism and makes it a crime, a wrong. In the face of dispersion, it asserts collectivity. Rather than a continuation of a left politics premised on cultivating a wide variety of issues and perspectives and then

[12] See my discussion in *The Communist Horizon*, London: Verso, 2012.

challenged to build affinities between them, Occupy asserted the economic division between the ninety-nine per cent and the one per cent as the basis for a new movement.[13]

Although the amplified individualism of communicative capitalism is a change from a society of mediating institutions, it isn't new. Marx and Engels note already in *The German Ideology* that 'competition isolates individuals, not only bourgeois but even more the proletarians, despite the fact that it brings them together. It takes a long time before these individuals can unite'.[14] Rosa Luxemburg similarly observes that the problem of social democracy in Russia was the atomized condition of the proletariat. Bourgeois society hadn't 'instilled in the working class the rudiments of political solidarity'.[15] It hadn't provided them the proper raw material, that is, the institutions, capacities, and expectations that would enable them to combine politically. Our conditions are also atomized, but differently. Ours is atomization as personalization, the atomization of the mobile, singular, and uncollected. In some ways, we have a surplus of raw materials for organization – rights to free speech and assembly, communication technologies, a modicum of literacy. The cost of the over-production of the means of communication has been a foreclosure of solidarity in the sense that too many of us seem to think that it's neither desirable nor necessary. In the US, we cling to individualism even as our ongoing proletarianization solidifies the gap between the one per cent and the rest of us. We have individuality without political subjectivity (which can only ever be collective).

[13] See my 'Claiming Division, Naming a Wrong', *Theory & Event*, Vol. 14, no. 4. 2011.

[14] Karl Marx, 'The German Ideology', *Selected Writings*, New York: Hackett, 1994, p. 142.

[15] Rosa Luxemburg, 'Organizational Questions of the Russian Social Democracy' (1904). http://www.marxists.org/archive/luxemburg/1904/questions-rsd/.

In 2008 the Left failed. There was a major crisis of capitalism inviting urgent response, but the Left was a no-show. The consequence has been more than bank bailouts and austerity. It's been the rise of the extreme Right as the most visible opponent of neoliberal governmental policies. The same crisis continues to deepen such that in the US, UK, and EU there is now *both* a new normal of intensifying inequality *and* a fundamental uncertainty as to the terms and conditions of this new normal. We don't know what this new condition that exceeds the political-economic settlements of welfare state and neoliberal state will be like – and this non-knowledge, this openness, is the opportunity for action, the space where we can push for one future over another, if we have the collective political will to do so. Is our setting one that can only be on-going cuts and austerity? Rising immizeration, reactive protest, and intensified police violence? Or can there be the collective steering of a world we create, use, and inhabit in common?

The crumbling of capitalist realism – the conviction that there is no alternative – has enabled ever more of us to see capitalism as the system of production through exploitation for the benefit of the few. But then what? It now seems that it's easier to imagine the end of capitalism than it is an organized Left. Left realists insist that collectivity is undesirable and impossible. It's undesirable because it excludes possibilities, effaces difference, and enforces discipline. It's impossible because we are so individuated, so singularized in our needs and ambitions, that we can't ever come together; coming together, we are told, is itself an illusion, a myth some use to manipulate others into fighting for their interests. Thus, today, amidst the uncertainties of late neoliberalism, even when we are fully conscious of our own exploitation, the deep inequity of the system in which we find ourselves, we either don't feel like we can do anything about it or we find ourselves participating in individuated, localized, or communicatively mediated activities without momentum, duration, or a capacity for political memory. People are immiserated and proletarianized and practically confront this immiseration and proletarianization alone.

Isolation, immiseration, and political disorganization also characterized the early decades of radical socialist movement. Marx, Engels, and Luxemburg all emphasize how competition means that workers tend to remain isolated, lack solidarity, and take a long time to unite. Left realists one-sidedly emphasize the objective dimension of our capitalist setting, failing to acknowledge the subjective dimension always part of the Marxist tradition.

There are differences between our time and that of the early years of revolutionary socialism. Rather than a period of working-class advance, ours is one of defeat. The rollback of the achievements of organized working-class struggle means austerity and privatization, particularly privatization accompanied by increases in brutality and exemption as practices formerly under public authority are turned over to personal power and the market. For us, authoritarianism is less that of centralized state power than it is of power decentralized, dispersed, and extended via private contracts, inter-bank and inter-agency cooperation, and the extensive network of treaties, agreements, and provisions enabling capital flow and global trade. National states act as the police force protecting the global capitalist class. So we encounter the fragmentation, dissolution, and decomposition of some elements of the state, and the concentration and intermeshing of other elements of states and markets, as in finance, security, and media. Capital as a class has worked to smash the bureaucratic state machine for us, to convince us that it is useless, even as it strengthens parts of it for its own ends.

We confront an uneven mix of centralizing and

decentralizing forces, in various combinations of state use of the market and market reliance on state. The state's operation as an instrument of class rule is tempered less by concessions forced on it by working-class struggle than it was forty years ago (although the social-democratic class compromise was itself not without political cost). Capital resurgence has reclaimed a great deal of ground, but it doesn't erase the fact of the prior struggles – indeed, our situation is particularly difficult because there has been a time in which basics such as housing, education, health, food, and work have been understood and treated as rights. Unfortunately, now is not that time.

Although the Left failed in 2008, new possibilities were emerging as activists and academics turned again to the idea of communism. These possibilities have been amplified by the new cycle of struggles we've seen in Wisconsin, Canada, Egypt, Spain, Greece, Turkey, the Occupy movement and other parts of the world. Part of the new appeal of the idea of communism is that 'communism' is the one word we have that bodes no compromise with capital *and* that asserts a powerful alternative. Linked to class struggle, the smashing of the bourgeois state, and the abolition of capitalists as a class, communism is more than social democratic compromise, post-structuralist pluralization, and anarchist insurrection. Instead of a politics thought primarily in terms of resistance, playful and momentary aesthetic disruptions, the immediate specificity of local projects, and struggles for hegemony within a democratic milieu, the horizon of communism impresses on us the necessity of eliminating capitalism and creating global practices and institutions of egalitarian cooperation. It turns us away from lifestyle changes, general inclusion, and momentary calls for awareness and toward militant opposition, tight organizational forms, and coordinated strategies for securing the people's control of the means of production. In contrast with anarchism's insistence on individuality, communism prioritizes solidarity.

For Marx, 'proletariat' names capitalism's self-creation of what destroys it. This 'what' that destroys capitalism is a collective subject, a force no longer dispersed in individual and local acts of smashing, sabotage, and disruption, but concentrated in solidarity. But *how* does this collective subject abolish capitalism? It can't be through destruction alone. The normal operation of the capitalist system is characterized by 'uncertainty and instability,' 'a series of periods of moderate activity, prosperity, over-production, crisis and stagnation'.[16] Contemporary capitalism has refined its capacity for wealth destruction: over 34 trillion dollars of market value was lost in the financial crisis of 2008. In the course of the recession that followed, the rich got richer and the poor got poorer: the top one per cent captured 121 per cent of the income gains made between 2009 and 2011.[17] Not only was the one per cent better able to weather the crisis than the rest of us, but it was also able to increase its share.

According to Marx, the capitalist cycle of creative destruction is brought to an end by the proletariat, but not by the working class organized as workers – they are already organized as workers in the factory, which enables them to become conscious of their material conditions and the need to combine into unions. The abolition of capitalism depends on the organization of the class as a *party*, a solidary political association that cuts across workplace, sector, region, and nation. The working class, *as a class*, is implicated in the success or stability of capitalism; capitalism configures its

[16] Karl Marx, *Capital*, edited by David McLellan, Oxford: Oxford University Press, 2008, p. 275.

[17] Bonnie Kavoussi,'Top One Percent Captured 121 Percent of All Income Gains During Recovery's First Year: Study', *Huffington Post*, 12 February, 2013.

struggles with the bourgeoisie. The party, however, takes as its horizon capitalism's supercession in communism. The party is necessary because class struggle is not simply economic struggle; it's political struggle.

Consider the famous passage from *The German Ideology*: 'We call communism the *real* movement which abolishes the present state of affairs'.[18] How should we understand this? Not as immediate insurrection or as prefiguration but rather as *the expansion of voluntary cooperation*. I say this because Marx explains that 'the conditions of this movement [we call communism] result from premises now in existence'. The premises he is discussing involve the multiplication of productive force through the cooperation of different individuals as this cooperation is determined by the division of labour and not as an effect of people's own united power. Abolishing determination by the division of labour is a matter of self-conscious collective action wherein cooperation is not forced, is not out of our control, but is instead willed commonly. Cooperation and concentration become self-conscious and willed rather than unconscious and determined. As the movement which abolishes the present state of affairs, communism expands *voluntary* cooperation.

In capitalist society this expansion of *voluntary* as opposed to compulsory cooperation happens through the party. An organization premised on solidarity, the party holds open a political space for the production of a common political will, a will irreducible to the capitalist conditions in which the majority of people find themselves forced to sell their labour power. Where work is obligatory, determined, membership in the party is voluntary, the willed formation of united power. Among its members, the party replaces competition with solidarity.

[18] 'The German Ideology', p. 120.

That class struggle is political means it exceeds the affirmation of people as workers with particular interests, extending to the critical assessment of this position as itself the result of inequality and exploitation. Differently put, the working class is a subject of capitalism. It is constrained within a field or discourse configured by and for capitalists as a class; it gets its position from within this field. So it might refuse and resist, sabotage and strike, but all these actions are still confined within a field given by capital, configured for its interests, and on its behalf. To be another kind of subject, the subject of another field, discourse, or politics, requires a break or twist, a shift to another field, the field of the party.[19]

The party is more than an outgrowth or extension of labour unions (this much at least should be uncontroversial given the importance of the peasantry in communist parties as well as the wide variety of sorts of groups founded by communist parties). The party is a form for abolishing capitalism and ushering in communism; it occupies the place of division, holding it open for a new collective political subject (for classical Marxism this was the proletariat; in *The Communist Horizon* I argue for the people as the rest of us – in each instance, though, subjectification is a possibility not an empirical given). At different points over the past hundred years, the party has attempted to abolish capitalism and usher in communism in various ways – revolutionary seizure of the

[19] Alain Badiou has something like this in mind in when he notes the internal split in the working class between its 'true political identity' and 'its latent corruption by bourgeois or imperialist ideas and practices' (8). He writes: 'the practical (historical) working class is always the contradictory unity of itself as proletariat and of it specific bourgeois inversion . . . This unity of opposites is determined .. by the general bourgeois space' (9). And, 'the bourgeoisie makes a subject' (42); 'the subjective effect of their force lies in the divided people' (42). Badiou, *Theory of the Subject*, London: Continuum, 2009.

state, participation in parliamentary processes, training of cadres and education of masses in order to be prepared when the time comes. The communist party has never been simply an organization aimed at achieving a set of economic reforms aimed at restraining capitalism's extremes and providing workers with welfare guarantees. That this is the case is clear when we note the justified sense of betrayal voiced by communists when their parties compromised and retreated. They feel betrayed because the party gave way on communist desire, the very desire its wide array of organizations hold open, the desire underpinning solidarity and comradeship.

The need for the party stems from the fact that the people are split between the ways we are given, positioned, within capitalism. We are situated within a field that tells us who we are and what we can be, that establishes the matrix of our desire, but that represses the truth of this field in class struggle. Capitalism strives to separate and individuate us, to instil in us the conviction that self-interest matters above all else, that freedom results from individual choices made for individual goals. It blocks from view the systemic determination of choices and outcomes, not to mention the power of collectives in rupturing these systems. When leftists assume the individualism of the dominant ideology, reiterating its emphases on uniqueness and trying to cultivate a politics out of individuated decisions, we undermine our own best impulses to collectivity and egalitarianism. The party asserts the truth of our division. It speaks from the position of this truth and offers another field of possibilities.[20] In opposition to capitalist desire, it opens up a terrain for the desire of a collective political subject. The party doesn't know everything. It provides a form for the knowledge we gain through

[20] Slavoj Žižek, *Revolution at the Gates*, London: Verso, 2002, pp. 185 – 89.

experience and analyse from the perspective of the communist horizon.

The array of classic party organizations – newspapers, literary magazines, clubs, trade associations, sports teams, schools, theatre troupes, women's groups, industry-focused councils, to mention but a few – reminds us that communist parties have always exceeded the binary of state and factory, actively engaging on multiple social, cultural, and economic fronts as elements of one struggle. As a red thread throughout the movements of the oppressed, communists connected divergent issues and experiences, enlarging them into a common world and mobilizing the collective desire for collectivity. Unlike standard parliamentary parties claiming representative authority, the work of the communist party involves substantialization, concentration, extension, and transference. Hence communist values of comradeship, solidarity, enthusiasm, and courage support the building of a political organization capable of responding in a revolutionary situation and enduring in less propitious times. Through the party, members push each other into modes of being and acting that appeared impossible before, when they were alone against capital and its state.

The problem the Left encounters today is less a matter of organizational details than it is of solidary political will. As the will emerges, people will figure out the structure in light of the challenges we face on particular fronts, challenges such as expanding militant pressure in ways that inspire and educate cadres while at the same time straining the resources of the state and breaking the confidence of the financial sector; abolishing private property and the capitalist banking system while advancing international coordination in an uneven environment; and increasing popular support of and developing a programme for common management of production, health, transportation, communication, food, housing, and education all in the setting of a changing climate, to mention but a few. Responding to these variable challenges generates new knowledge that can be integrated and shared. There is no reason to assume that every component of the party must have the same structure. A global alliance of the radical Left, or, better, a new party of communists, can be knit together from the concentrated forces of already existing groups: militants skilled at direct action, artists adept with symbols and slogans, parties experienced at organizing, issue groups knowledgeable about specific areas of concern, mutual aid networks addressing basic needs. Such a concentration would let people who want to be engaged in radical politics but aren't sure what to do have a place to go, a place to start.

More importantly, such a concentration would amplify specific and local achievements as collective victories in the broader struggle for communism. At the most minimal level, if we are to have a chance of taking power, of reformatting the basic conditions under which we live and work, we need to share a name in common as a fundamental marker of division. We need to know who we can trust and to extend the bonds of trust beyond local ties and small networks. An absence of solidarity may be the biggest challenge right now insofar as without solidarity a common will cannot emerge. Defeat, betrayal, fear, as well as on-going patterns of sexism, racism, and homophobia have made us deeply suspicious. A party helps deal with this through explicit criteria for membership and expectations for members. Cellular structure can help ensure that each person is connected to a known group of others to whom she is accountable. Delegating tasks lets us acknowledge different strengths and skills. Trusting others' skills and knowledge is essential if we are to form ourselves into a political force capable of addressing global capital.

I have suggested a name in common and some basic structural components involving membership organized in cells, delegating tasks, and following a common purpose. The idea behind this rudimentary sketch is that the party is a political form of commitment, a solidarity requiring of members a willingness to put aside endless self-assertion and admit that pulling together is more important than insisting on one's own uniqueness.

To conclude, the question of the party, the organizational question, is being once again pushed to the fore. As movements encounter problems with horizontal and leaderless visions of political organization, as they confront the failures of protests and occupations to endure, as they admit that resistance is futile and revolution is necessary, they force us again to make and to be a party of communists. They dare us to enact a political association that does not imagine itself as the whole of community as idealized friendship but that instead rests on fighting side by side for an emancipated, egalitarian political, economic, and social formation.

REMEMBERING THE OCTOBER REVOLUTION BY REBUILDING THE SOCIALIST IMAGINATION

Prabir Purkayastha

To remember the October Revolution meaningfully today, we need to address a couple of fundamental questions first. How do we overthrow capitalism given its new forms, and the fragmentation of the global working class? And to this end, what socialist agenda do we put forward before the people today?

To begin with, we need to understand the current structure of the production process created by capital. To articulate the political challenges of the working class, we need to analyse the changing form of capitalist production.

THE FORDIST PARADIGM

The 20th century created a production system built on economies of scale. This refers to large, vertically integrated factories, what we call the Fordist paradigm. The automation technologies were geared to create such factories, and one of the first of these was Ford Motors, hence the name.

These vertically integrated factories subjugated the worker to the machine and the assembly line. Charlie Chaplin portrays this process brilliantly in the film *Modern Times*. But these factories also made it possible for the working class to organize at the factory floor level and introduce its politics at the factory floor. Given the size of the factory, it was possible to build very large unions. And very large factory level unions enabled the working class to halt production and create a political impact. Thus the factory floor gave rise to, and led, the politics of the working class in the 20th century.

The production technology of the 20th century favoured backward and forward integration, and these large, vertically integrated factories were also replicated under socialism. This is the case with the Soviet Union. After the October Revolution, it is true that the socialist system was built on a similar system of economies of scale, facilitating centrally planned economies or the command economy.

Automation played a key role in these integrated factories. In *Modern Times*, automation reduces the worker, in effect, to an appendage of the machine. Technology is not neutral between the classes. It obviously plays the role of subordinating the worker to capital. By introducing a certain kind of automation on the factory floor, it helps the capitalist class to subjugate the working class. It also produced its own counterpoint – the counterforce of workers organizing at that level. While it helped capital create large factories that dominated production, it also created its antipode – the organized working-class.

POST-FORDIST PRODUCTION SYSTEM

With the next technological change, the factory floor as a production system begins to break up. Technology is decentralized; it is de-scaled; and the factory floor is fragmented. The Information Technology (IT) industry brings in the automation of the production process. It also creates the possibility of subordinating the entire supply chain – from the raw materials to the final product – and integrating it all through IT. The factory floor can be broken up and distributed to different locations. We have global products of which different parts are produced in different places, then brought together to be assembled in a final location.

Consider one company that produces such decentralized products – Apple. All the designs come from Apple; it decides what the components should be; while the product is manufactured and assembled by Foxconn. The product is then distributed to different markets under the brand name Apple. Apple controls the technology and also the market, because of its branding and its control over distribution.

This is a significant change, this possibility of subordinating the entire production processes and dispersing it to various locations. And so the political strength of the working-class gets fragmented. The new challenge for the working class is that it is no longer possible to organize easily in one place. The factory floor is no longer the primary focus of resistance. How can resistance work then, in times when the traditional factory floor breaks up, and even workers are not easily recognisable as workers in an earlier sense?

MCDONALDIZATION OF LABOUR

Well-known Marxist David Harvey suggests that the Left has not been able to organize employees of workplaces such as McDonalds because of a failure to recognise them as part of the working class. I would argue that this 'McDonaldization of labour' is only part of the problem. As Marxists, or as political activists, we do recognise the need to organize all workers, wherever they are. But it is difficult to organize workers who are transient; who take up such jobs for a year or two, then go somewhere else; who do not see such places or such jobs as permanent. These are the difficulties of organizing workers in the McDonald-like employment sector.

This kind of transient labour is, of course, not peculiar to McDonald. We find transient labour in different industries across the world. The capitalist system, and the technology which supports the fragmentation of the working class, understands this. Technology is not neutral: it works in different ways to support the capitalist class. One such understanding is that in breaking up of the factory floor, it is also breaking up the working class resistance and this is something which will help capital dominate the workers. So it is not by accident that the factory floor has been fragmented.

INTELLECTUAL PROPERTY AND THE RISE OF APPLE

In the 20th century, the capitalist class appropriated the surplus value created on the factory floor. In the more complex situation today, the surplus appropriated by capital today, is not only the surplus value created on the factory floor, but also the redistribution of the surplus through the mechanism of intellectual property.

Apple has the largest market capitalization in world. It is worth 800 billion dollars in market capital terms, more than the GDP of many countries.[1] However, Apple itself does not produce anything. It does not even have a factory. Instead, it has intellectual property. It has the designs, the patents, the copyrights; it has the Apple brand. It controls the production cycle through the technology used to make Apple products; and it controls the market through the Apple brand. Thus the production process can be fragmented all over the world.

Of course, Apple is not the only company using intellectual property to create monopolies and amass wealth. Pharmaceutical and media companies have been doing this for a long time. Apple has just taken it to a different level, so that it has become the largest company in the world.

HOW TO ORGANIZE LABOUR TODAY AND THE VANGUARD ROLE OF THE WORKING CLASS

More than fifty per cent of the members of all large trade unions today come from the unorganized sector. This

[1] As of April 2017, Apple's market cap would rank it as 17th in global GDP rankings. http://statisticstimes.com/economy/countries-by-projected-gdp.php

is the small-scale sector, where workers are organized at the industry level and not the factory floor. This also applies to construction workers, temporary, casual labourers working at different places, food industry workers and such.

All of us recognise the importance of organizing the working class as a whole. But how do we it? How do we respond to the fragmentation of the factory floor and the creation of a transient workforce?

The challenge of organizing the working class demands a shift. It is no longer enough to organize the workers at the point of production. We need now to look at the production cycle as a whole. We have to organize workers at the point of production; and at the point of consumption, which is the fight against the brands, intellectual property, the rent, economy; we also need to organize them at the point of reproduction of capital – the reproduction of workers – which takes place in the neighbourhoods, the place where workers live.

The working class movement today needs to organize the workers across the industries: as metal workers, construction workers, *anganvadi* workers, etc. The action of the workers will then be across the entire industry, not just in a factory. This is certainly much harder to do than organizing in factories.

There is also the need to organize the workers as consumers and against intellectual property. The movement against intellectual property – in pharmaceuticals, software, music, books, films – is an integral part of the fight against global capital. These industries survive on extraction of monopoly rent from the people, a monopoly built on patents or copyright. Once a medicine goes off patents, it can go down to one twentieth of its price. In the case of AIDS, the western drug companies were charging $10,000 for a year's supply against generics from India costing only a fraction – $350. A device such as a smartphone is covered by thousands of software patents. India not allowing software patents means that much cheaper mobile phones can be made available to the people. The struggle against copyrights and patenting of software has huge implications for the people and therefore such struggles are very much a part of the struggle of the working class against capital.

How do you reproduce labour, how do you reproduce workers? The reproduction of labour means cheap electricity, water, health and education for its children. The capitalist system did not build public infrastructure such as roads, electricity, and telecom, introduce education and public health, as gifts to the people. These were the hard won rights of the working class, as was the 8-hour day. All these elements are today under attack by the capitalist system.

The neoliberal state's attack on public infrastructure is a part of this onslaught of global capital. While the electricity workers fight against privatization of electricity, they also need to mobilize the consumers who, after privatization, are going to pay with much higher prices of electricity. Similarly, the municipal workers must lead the struggle against the privatization of water. The privatization of water supplies in Cochabamba, the third largest city in Bolivia, was fought by a coalition of union workers (Federation of the Workers), townspeople and peasant irrigators.

All over the world, public health systems are under attack. In India, as in many other countries, health insurance and private hospitals are replacing public hospitals and clinics. Private education is supplanting the public education system built after independence. The struggle of the people against privatization of health and education is very much a part of the working class struggle.

The struggle against the neoliberal state's attack on the people needs also to be fought where the people live. It is not enough for the working class to organize the workers in their place of work. Therefore, local struggle committees are as much of a part of the larger struggle of the workers against capital as the unions.

The complexity of the working class movement today is that the struggle against capital was relatively simpler in the 20th century. It has become much more complex in the 21st century, as the challenge of the working class today is not just to organize the workers at the point of production but at the point of production, at the point of re-production, and at the point of consumption. All these three elements need to be brought together and fought.

What is the role of the organized working class in such struggles? Some theorists suggest that we do not need organized working class politics or a vanguard role for the working class any longer. For instance, Antonio Negre and Michael Hardt talk about the *Empire*, and not about imperialism.[2] They argue that the empire can be organically replaced by distributed struggles all over the place. And such forms of struggles do not need vanguard parties, or an organized working class.

Such a formulation neglects the fundamental nature of the bourgeois state and its centralized nature. No amount of diffused struggle can organically change the state. We need mass and class struggles to challenge the bourgeois state and replace it with a working-class state. It is only the working-class, which has the emancipatory potential, and the politics, to be able to see the capitalist system as a whole. Ultimately, it is from a location within the production system that we understand the capitalist system in a fundamental sense. This view of the system does not happen at the point of consumption or at the point of reproduction of the workers. Hence the politics of the working-class must till originate where things are produced, the place from where we have the best view of

[2] Michael Hardt and Antonio Negri, *Empire*, Cambridge: Harvard University Press, 2001.

the system. The vanguard still remains the organized working-class at the factory level; and that is why the need to privilege the organized working class.

IMPERIALISM AND GLOBAL SOLIDARITY

The second challenge that the Left faces is the global struggle against war and imperialism.

Capitalism today is much more integrated, much more powerful than we think it is. There has been much discussion about the weakening of imperialism, the imperialist agenda and about American-led imperialist hegemony. The emergence of BRICS has been described as an element of this weakening, though not as a socialist or progressive alternative, but as a challenge to the centralized hegemony of American imperialism.

There are two contradictions in this formulation. While it is true that American or western hegemony has, in some sense, weakened with the emergence of BRICS and other capitalist blocks,, we still have the Western capitalist system in which Americans are the lynchpins, working as a unified imperialist block. While the western economic hegemony might have weakened, we cannot underestimate the destructive military power of the US. The US may find it difficult to control countries after it has occupied them; but it can occupy them very quickly. Afghanistan was occupied in one week, Iraq in two weeks. The US and its allies also destroyed Libya. The consequence has been the destabilization of different countries in North Africa. There are the examples of Syria and Yemen. All these show how the US destructive power is actually increasing, while its ability to control them – after it destroys these countries – has weakened. So the US today, in its phase of weakening of hegemony, still poses a destructive threat to the world.

Thus international solidarity against US imperialism – global solidarity – and against war has become even more important. And here is the problem. The international working-class solidarity that had existed no longer exists today. Different Left forces are emerging; existing Left parties in many places are losing their strength. The old and new Left formations do not know each other well. For instance, those who have had links with Palestine for a number of years do not know the new forces emerging there. The Indian state, which did support the Palestinian liberation struggle, is now taking a completely different direction. Those of us in the Left today need to reinvigorate and re-establish our ties with the Palestinian movements.

It is clear that an international solidarity movement has to be built, or to be precise, re-built. The World Social Forum (WSF) was an attempt in this direction. The WSF slogan 'Another world is possible', helped bring all of us together. But it did not provide a real vision for the kind of world we want to build. WSF got a number of movements together, creating a basis for global solidarity. But it did not produce the kind of solidarity movements we need today. This is the second crisis of the working class: while global capital seems to be quite well organized and able to coordinate its policies – for example on Greece – the Left movement, the working class movement, does not have that unity. Creating this unity, building that solidarity, is our task at the global level.

THE CHALLENGE OF THE SOCIALIST IMAGINATION

Perhaps it is the third challenge which is the most important. After the fall of the Soviet Union, there has been a crisis of the socialist imagination. In this period of crisis, we talk about the limitations of the Soviet experiment and later of the Chinese experiment. We are critical – depending on our political stream – on how they deviate from the socialist path. These 'deviations' have been described as social imperialism, bureaucratic capitalism, state capitalism, or bureaucratic socialism. But these critics of the socialist experiments have not offered, concrete ideas on what could have been done instead in that phase of socialism.

Keeping in mind the context of 20th century socialism and its limitations, that the command economy was the consequence of a production technology that privileged economies of scale and therefore, vertical and horizontal integration. When we come to the 21st century, we have to build our new emancipatory model of 21st century socialism. For this to happen, we have to envision the socialist system of production in the 21st century.

Without such an emancipatory model of socialism, we would limit our imagination in the fight against capitalism. No system falls because of all the problems of such a system. Even in physics or natural sciences, no theory gets overthrown by its contradictions; it gets overthrown only when a new theory addresses those contradictions and resolves them. Similarly, we have to construct a vision of the socialist system – that can, as a system of production, express itself in different ways, even within the womb of the neoliberal capitalism.

And this vision must be effectively communicated to the people.

To build such a vision, we need to probe the nascent forms of socialist production. This calls for a critical examination of what capitalism is doing to production. If capitalism can de-skill technology, break up and fragment the work place, is it possible for us to bring intellect workers, say those who produce designs for Apple, together with the manual workers who manufacture Apple products? Can we get that knowledge that exists with intellect workers; and combine it with the existing small-scale production – who produce a whole lot of goods in either a petty commodity production mode, or as ancillaries to the major brand names? Can we get them together to build a different system of production within the existing structure? Can we weaken capitalism's control over knowledge and over brands? Can we start fighting all these today – and not wait till we seize state power?

Our earlier slogan was 'Think global, fight local'. This is not enough today. We have to think global, but we also have to fight globally. We cannot fight the capitalist system at one place; that place can be abandoned by the capitalist for another. Capital has become, in some sense, footloose, because it owns the intellectual property, the designs, the software, the distribution system, the brand name. It does not care where its products are manufactured. Apple can abandon Foxconn and go to somebody else, located in a completely different place, with very little loss. Foxconn, merely manufactures the Apple products. Not surprisingly, of the iPhone price, Apple's profits are 58.5 per cent, Foxconn's 14.3 per cent profit, while the workers are paid, as wages, only 1.8 per cent of the iPhone price.[3] Apple can offer high wages to a small number of intellect workers who produce the designs and the software, while the bulk of the workers producing the actual phone are paid a pittance.

Can the Left fight Apple not simply by organizing workers but building smartphones through producers' cooperatives that bring together intellect workers and the workers who make the phones? With free software movements and peer-to-peer production movements, this is possible today. Can the Left and the local governments that may be under its sway, lead such efforts?

This is not to argue that the workers' cooperatives will

[3] Christian Fuchs, 'Digital Labor and Imperialism', *Monthly Review*, January 2016.

gradually replace capitalism without the need of seizing state power. My argument here is that we need to think about how to combine our socialist vision of the future – the kind of production system, the kind of distribution, the kind of ownership – and *begin demonstrating* parts of these here and now.[4] We can then provide a platform for local Left governments, give them certain tasks of building and demonstrating proto-socialist alternatives, even within the existing constraints. Otherwise, Left governments have the danger of becoming merely better caretakers of the capitalist system than the capitalist parties themselves. We may not have all the answers, but we need to start thinking on how we can built an alternative system of production, and start, experimenting on it today.

Repeated capitalist crisis is integral to capitalism: it will continue to be there as long as capitalism exists. As long as capitalism is not overthrown, it will always get over its crisis by expanding in different ways, finding new commodities; at the current moment, it finds personal data as the new commodity; it expands continuously into new dimensions, through dispossessions, through enclosure of the commons, and so on. Unless we have an alternative system in place, at least in our imagination, capitalism cannot be overthrown. Our task is to see how to overthrow capitalism, but that cannot be done unless we combine it with an emancipatory vision of *our* socialism and our socialist imagination. This is how we should remember the October Revolution, not through empty homage but by rebuilding our revolutionary vision.

[4] For a study of an important socialist cooperative, see T. M. Thomas Isaac and Michelle Winters, *Constructing Alternatives: The Story of a Workers' Society in Kerala*, New Delhi: LeftWord Books, forthcoming.

MARXISM, FEMINISM & REVOLUTION

Shahrzad Mojab

Three years before the Russian Revolution, the capitalist states went to war, bringing immense destruction of life and property to every corner of the world. The First World War recurred on a more destructive scale within the life span of a generation, and it has continued to our day in a region from the Balkans to the Middle East to Africa, and threatens other parts of the world. While states, media, academia, and many non-state organizations have a stake in commemorating the First World War, it is unlikely if anyone will remember what Mary White Ovington (1865 – 1951), a socialist and feminist, said four months before the launch of the mass slaughter:

> Socialism and Feminism are the two greatest movements of to-day. The one aims to abolish poverty, the other to destroy servitude among women. Both are world movements. No matter how backward the nation may be that you visit, you will find your revolutionist there preaching that poverty is unnecessary, and that a great organization is working to destroy private capital and to build a co-operative commonwealth. And throughout western civilization, and even in the heart of the Orient, you also find the woman revolutionist telling her enslaved sisters of the effort among women to attain their freedom, to gain the right to live, not according to man's, but according to their own conception of happiness and right. Ideas fly swiftly about the globe, and we are learning to think on the lines not of family or nation or race but of common interests and common suffering.[1]

Ovington emphasized that 'the relation of Feminism to

[1] M. W. Ovington, 'Socialism and the Feminist Movement', *New Review: A Weekly Review of International Socialism*, Vol. 2, no. 3, 1914, p. 143

Socialism is a matter of profound importance to many women Socialists'. She was right. Three years earlier, socialist women had launched 8 March as International Working Women's Day (IWWD), and three years later the first socialist state was established – and women played an active role in it. On the theoretical front, twenty years before Ovington, Frederich Engels had published *The Origin of Family, Private Property and the State* (1884), and years before this major milestone, August Bebel's *Woman and Socialism* (1879) was published. I do not intend to write the history of relations between feminism and socialism or Marxism. It is well known that this relationship has been both conflictual and constructive, and today they are evidently apart. Floyd Dell, while defending Ovington who had been criticized by an anti-feminist, wrote, 'If there is no necessary connection between Feminism and Socialism, it may yet be advisable to invent one'.[2]

Socialism and feminism have changed radically since Ovington, but her ideas, simple and significant as they are, remain on the agenda of many who yearn for an end to both 'poverty' and 'servitude'. The October 1917 revolution in Russia was for many the realization of this dream. This revolution made Marxism the dominant trend in the theory and practice of socialism, and divided the world into socialist and capitalist camps. However, in spite of great leaps towards women's emancipation, the socialist experiments of the last century came to an end when capitalism was restored first in the Soviet Union (1956) and, within two decades, in China (1976).[3] The collapse of the Soviet Union and Eastern

[2] F. Dell, 'Socialism and Feminism', *New Review: A Weekly Review of International Socialism*, Vol. 2, no. 6, 1914, p. 353.

[3] The building of socialism and the restoration of capitalism constitute processes of struggle on many fronts, and cannot be traced to an exact date. However, in the case of the USSR, the Twentieth Congress of the Communist Party in 1956 became a watershed after Nikita Khrushchev launched, in a 'secret report', a major theoretical and ideological

Europe in the late 1980s and early 1990s was trumpeted by the bourgeoisie as the 'end of history', one in which socialism (almost always conflated with 'communism' in the media and in popular parlance) was buried and capitalism emerged triumphant. During the past century, every success of socialism had attracted many to the cause of freedom, and each retreat has resulted in the turning away of many enthusiasts.[4] After the fall of the Soviet Union, which in its last decades was critiqued by many Marxists as a 'state capitalist' or 'social imperialist' country, the theory and practice of socialism and with it of Marxism came under a new wave of scrutiny and rejection by, among others, feminists. Today, many advocates of capitalism

....

shift, which the Communist Party of China assessed as a project of restoration of capitalism. The conflict over this shift led, by 1963 – 64, to the first major split in the post-1917 international communist movement. The party in China initiated the Great Proletarian Cultural Revolution (1966 – 68, and continuing unofficially until 1976) as a means to prevent the restoration of capitalism in the way it had happened in the USSR. In both 1956 and 1976, the architects of restoration resorted to violence against the advocates of socialism. Before 1956, critics had explained the limitations of Soviet socialism as a product of bureaucratization (state capitalism), the personality or psychology of Stalin (dictatorship), or the retarded development of productive forces (economism). Mao provided a different explanation by emphasizing the nature of socialism as a class society, its transitional position between capitalism and communism, the prominence of class struggle especially in the party, the role of political and ideological line, and the determining nature of the superstructure in the course of transition from capitalism to socialism. In China much more than in the USSR, restoration happened in the wake of intensive political and ideological struggles between 'socialist roaders' and 'capitalist roaders'.

[4] For instance, six years after the formation of the People's Republic of China (in October 1949), Simone de Beauvoir visited the country and wrote in detail about the progress made in the life of the Chinese people, especially women. To give another example, Julia Kristeva visited China in the wake of the Cultural Revolution and depicted the Chinese Revolution as a 'women's revolution'. Simone de Beauvoir, *The Long March: An Account of Modern China*, London: Phoenix, 2001 and Julia Kristeva, *About Chinese Women*, New York: Marion Boyars, 1991.

justify the way this socio-economic system produces wealth as well as poverty, hunger, and destruction of the environment.

Feminism's trajectory has not been as tumultuous, but not quite dissimilar either. Unlike Marxism, which rose to state power and guided the construction of socialism for a few decades in a number of countries, feminism contributed prominently to reforming patriarchy through women's movements for equal rights within the contours of the state. While Marxism was hesitantly tolerated in the margins of capitalist academe, feminism spread out, by the early 1970s, from the privacy of individual theorists and the publicity of street politics to degree-granting programmes, and has grown into a credible, if still resisted, international realm of knowledge. Feminist scholarship has seriously challenged the patriarchal nature of all previous knowledge. In stark contrast to Marxism, it comes today with hundreds of women's and gender studies programmes, hundreds of academic journals, and a powerful publishing industry, enabling it to train new generations of feminist scholars and intelligentsia. However, if Marxism was derailed by the 'socialist' state that was meant to plan its own 'withering away,' feminism has been, according to some feminists, co-opted by its rise to academic status. Today, while gender and women's studies programmes proliferate in higher education in Western countries, anti-feminism is hegemonic in popular culture and the mass media wherein feminism is rejected, even by some self-styled feminists, as 'extremist' and as exhibiting an 'anti-male bias'.[5] In other contexts, for example, in Iran and Turkey, there is considerable interest in feminist theory and research as a venue of struggle against the patriarchal gender politics of the state and its anti-feminist

[5] R. Hammer, *Anti-feminism and Family Terrorism*, Lanham: Rowman & Littlefield, 2002.

agenda. In Iran, the Islamic theocracy makes use of the anti-feminism of American Christianity.[6]

The interest in merging the theoretical positions of Marxism and feminism, which has not subsided since the beginning of the last century, is fuelled by their prominence as two major emancipatory projects.[7] This political affinity is, however, constrained by divergent theoretical commitments that are themselves political and ideological. Theoretically, Marxism and feminism have never been so far apart as at present.

The idea of a society without gender oppression and class exploitation predates both feminism and Marxism. Indeed, conflicts over gender and class weave together the entirety of human history. Put in the span of the long history of *homo sapiens* (a few hundred thousand years), gender and class conflicts (as well as private property, family, trade, war, armies, states, laws, writings) are social constructions of recent origins, dating back about eight to ten millennia. This nearness in time invites a simple but crucial question: Why do class and patriarchal gender relations survive and even thrive in spite of widespread resistance and theoretical advances?

Feminism is both the product and a producer of the Enlightenment and its bourgeois democratic revolutions, whereas Marxism emerged in the context of the assumption of power by the bourgeoisie and the rise of working class.

[6] S. Mojab, 'The State and Women's Studies: The Islamization-Indigenization of Anti-Feminism', *Iran Nameh*, Vol. 29, no. 4 [in Persian].

[7] Marxism's preoccupation with women's emancipation is widely acknowledged. Michèle Barrett, for instance, has noted that 'Outside feminist thought itself there is no tradition of critical analysis of women's oppression that could match the incisive attention given to this question by one Marxist thinker after another'. M. Barrett, 'Feminism', *A Dictionary of Marxist Thought*, T. Bottomore, et. al., Cambridge: Harvard University Press, 1983, p. 164.

Two *class* positions, one seeking emancipation within the legal and political frameworks of the capitalist system and the other seeking the same through the negation of bourgeois relations, separate the two. Summing up the experience of the first two years of socialist revolution, Lenin noted that 'one of the principal distinguishing features of capitalism' is that it 'combines formal equality with economic and, consequently, social inequality.'[8] Even formal equality, to the extent it has been achieved in capitalist societies, did not come without resistance. It took a century of women's organized struggle to persuade the state to grant them suffrage rights. Although socialist countries readily granted women extensive legal equality and took steps towards their economic and social equality, the transformation of gender relations was marked by compromise and retreat, and patriarchy survived through to the restoration of capitalism.

Marxist theory has provided clues for understanding the intricacies involved in the dismantling of class and patriarchy. Society is a whole, and class, gender, race, religion, and other social phenomena, far from being independent, exist in relationships of determination and conflict as a system, a social formation, or a mode of production. Equally significant is the way this system and its components persist only in the course of reproducing themselves. In his study of capitalist production, for example, Marx noted that 'When viewed . . . as a connected whole, and as flowing on with incessant renewal, every social process of production is, at the same time, a process of reproduction.'[9] From this perspective, patriarchy may be seen as a connected whole, a social process for producing and reproducing the gender hierarchy characterized by male

[8] V. I. Lenin, *On the Emancipation of Women*, Moscow: Progress Publishers, 1982, p. 84.

[9] Karl Marx, *Capital*, Moscow: Progress Publishers, 1983, volume 1, p. 531.

domination. Male power, much like class rule, is exercised through both coercion and consent; consent is created through family, religion, ideology, culture, language, literature, art, folklore, education, and all other cultural institutions, while physical violence is perpetrated by males, the police, armies, the law, and courts. There is no clear-cut separation between the two; the family, for instance, perpetrates violence while it generates consent. Dialectics predicts that such a system will be fraught with contradictions, with the two genders existing in relations of conflict and dependence. Class, race, and religion, among other social formations, also endure only if they reproduce themselves. It happens that these dynamics of producing and reproducing, indispensable in any system, cannot be adequately accounted for by the idea that class, gender, race, or sexuality 'intersect'.[10]

The experience of socialism in the last century revealed the complexities of negating the capitalist system's dynamics of production and reproduction and replacing it with that of a communist system. Socialism was, in Marx's understanding, a long transition period between capitalism and communism, in which classes and capitalist relations would persist in conflict with communist relations that have to be consciously created. It involves the dismantling of one social system by building its opposite. This transition for Marx was to involve nothing less than what he called the abolition of class distinctions, 'the abolition of all the relations of production on which they rest', 'the abolition of all the social relations that correspond to these relations of production,' and 'the revolutionizing

[10] D. Aguilar, 'From Triple Jeopardy to Intersectionality: The Feminist Perplex', *Comparative Studies of South Asia, Africa and the Middle East*, Vol. 32, no. 2, 2012 and Himani Bannerji, *Inventing Subjects: Studies in Hegemony, Patriarchy and Colonialism*, London: Anthem, 2001.

of all the ideas that result from these social relations'.[11] Such intervention in social reality calls for some theoretical breakthrough. Politically, such disruptions in the dynamics of production and reproduction invite hostility, both nationally and internationally, from those who have a stake in the survival of capitalism. If this conflict is visibly political, dealing with relations of power, it is no less significant in the realms of philosophy and ideology. This struggle is what Marxist textbooks call 'the fundamental question of philosophy', that is, the dialectics of matter and consciousness, as well as other dialectical relations such as those between necessity and freedom, essence and phenomenon, and universal and particular.[12] Ideologically, the question of alternatives to capitalism drops anchor in class positions.

Feminist theory, in all its diversity today, is not committed to the negation of capitalism, and some theorists do not see gender relations as a system (patriarchy) while others reject the idea of women's emancipation or liberation as 'grand narratives'. Even more reductionist is feminism's delinking of gender relations and capitalism and reducing gender to questions of culture. This is a feminism that finds solace in discarding the conceptual framework of twentieth-century women's movements, including the concepts of oppression, exploitation, subjugation, subordination, solidarity, and internationalism at a time when religious and market fundamentalisms are engaged in a world-wide 'war on women'. These developments cannot be explained in theoretical terms only; these theoretical positions are not replacements of paradigms or the falling and rising of 'waves' in feminist theory and politics. While feminism has indeed made enormous

[11] Karl Marx, 'The Class Struggles in France, 1848 to 1850', *Selected Works*, Moscow: Progress Publishers, 1969, Vol. 1.

[12] For more on this, see *Educating from Marx: Race, Gender and Learning*, ed. S. Carpenter and S. Mojab, New York: Palgrave, 2011.

contributions to our understanding of gender relations since the theoretical twists and turns of the 1980s, its delinking of capitalism and patriarchy is a political undertaking that undermines theoretical gains in our understanding of gender relations. This politics ensures the anchoring of feminism in liberalism and – at best – democratic theory and their links to the market.

It is well known that the economic determinist trend in Marxism and, more evidently, in communist movements has reduced gender relations to class relations. This reading of Marxism, often anti-dialectical in its method, is based on conflating class with gender and reducing the political to the economic. It fails to appreciate that class is not gender and gender is not class, but that the struggle over gender relations (patriarchy) is a political struggle among and within classes. It is, thus, not difficult to find different class positions disagreeing on how and to what extent the patriarchal regime should be transformed. The class reductionist position is, however, not primarily a product of the unfamiliarity of Marxists with feminism; rather, it is related to their undialectical understanding of Marxism. Hence, while the vast knowledge produced by feminism is indispensible for the renewal of Marxism and the communist movement, a new synthesis is unlikely to happen without a dialectical approach to Marxism itself.

The political character of the struggle over two major historical divides, gender and class, is evident also in the perseverance of anti-feminism and anti-communism and their ubiquity. It is also inscribed in the endless conflicts within each theoretical perspective, Marxism and feminism, and between the two. Not a question of sectarianism, the politics of theorization is one of splits, ruptures, zigzags, advances, and retreats rather than a linear march forward. This is the case if only because, dialectically speaking, one always divides into two. I see in the diversity or richness of today's feminist knowledge seeds of conservatism. Reflecting on my lived experience of the last five decades, I have seen how, in confronting patriarchy, the major element of consciousness, that is, theory, lags behind 'material reality' or matter, and at times stays in conflict with it. For instance, I find feminism's culturalization of gender relations and its abandoning of projects of emancipation at odds with the offensive of capitalism on women throughout the world.

I have realized, following Marx, that we make our own history, but not under circumstances chosen by us; we are constrained by circumstances already existing and given and transmitted from the past. This dialectic reverberates in another one: 'Freedom' is, according to Hegel, the recognition of 'necessity.' But necessity, that is, circumstances of the past and present, cannot be changed through recognition or interpretation only. Contemporary feminist theory engages in interpretation but, as Marx said in another context, the challenge is also to change reality. In other words, transformation occurs when matter transforms into consciousness and consciousness into matter. Feminist consciousness is the outcome of the rise of women as a new social and political force and their determination to change the material reality of oppressive and unjust gender relations. This consciousness has, through the practice of women's movements worldwide, changed gender relations through struggles for 'rights,' but has failed to dismantle the hierarchy of gender relations.

The academic environment in which I have lived, first as a graduate student from 1984 and then as a faculty member from 1993, is a record of far-reaching changes in the knowledge and power relations of higher education. Back in Illinois after having experienced the defeat of an important revolution,

I wanted to write and talk about women, students, and nationalities under theocratic rule. The women of Iran were now a topic of interest in media and popular culture, human rights and women's rights groups, and soon in courses and the publishing industry. I wanted to talk about the relationship between state, ideology, patriarchy, religion, class, ethnicity, nationalism, and feminism. But, I was often told, encouraged, and frequently demanded to speak about my 'identity', 'body', or 'culture'. I was being constructed as a 'Muslim' woman and the region of the word that I came from as a 'Muslim society'. Before 1979, I was never considered or treated as a 'Muslim' woman. Post-1979, a host of theoretical claims, old and new, trapped me into an identity that did not belong to me and that I could not identify with. Cultural relativism, identity politics, post-structuralism, post-modernism, and other turns and shifts to language and culture worked to confine my horizons to 'authenticity', 'religion', 'nativism', and 'ethnicity'. In this theoretical environment, political belonging to internationalism, feminism, socialism, communism, atheism, or secularism is not welcomed, especially for those who appear to be the 'other'.

I resisted this theoretical conservatism, which was in line with the political conservatism of neo-liberalism and which was spreading by the early 1990s to every corner of the world. While this perspective was, in my understanding, serving the interests of capital and religion, many individuals and oppressed groups picked up the language of belonging and identity. Theorists inspired all, from women to students to oppressed aboriginal, racial, ethnic and national groups, to avoid 'grand narratives' of freedom and class struggle. While capitalism systemically evades borders and creates new ones, and women's movements and feminist consciousness are increasingly international, theorists push for a 'micropolitical' understanding in this globalizing world. Since this internationalization is, indeed, difficult to deny, it is often presented as 'transnationalism', a conceptual frame that remains within the boundaries of nationalism.[13]

Moving from the conservatism of non-Marxist social theory to the conformism of the Marxist Left, of which I was part, I focus now on the contradiction between their theory and practice of gender politics. Communist groups in Iran, as elsewhere, have been the most persistent advocates of women's rights. However, their theoretical approach to patriarchy reduced gender oppression to class exploitation, and found the solution to oppression in a socialist revolution which would overthrow capitalism and, with it, patriarchal oppression. They failed to appreciate that gender is not class and that exploitation is a relationship between capitalists and workers whereas male oppression is a trans-class political relationship in which men of all classes, including workers, oppress women. Also, they failed to grasp the dialectics of this struggle: While gender cannot be reduced to class, the struggle over gender relations, that is, the dismantling of patriarchy, is inescapably political and, therefore, constitutes class struggle. Thus, the left's prioritizing of improving workers' lives and of independence from imperialist domination over women's emancipation is a political position, one that underestimates the crucial role of women in revolutionary change, and by doing so it overlooks the destructive nature of the exercise of power by the male gender. Similarly, the Shah's denigration of women and Khomeini's Islamization of gender relations are as political as their suppression of workers, peasants, students, minorities, artists, and journalists. The Left failed

[13] *Scattered Hegemonies: Postmodernity and Trasnnationalism*, eds. Inderpal Grewal and Caren Kaplan, Minneapolis: University of Minnesota, 1994.

to understand that women's oppression has been crucial in creating the conditions for capitalist/imperialist exploitation of all working people. This I regard as an economistic/workerist approach among most Left tendencies.

Eonomistic theory linked with nationalistic understanding of imperialism did not allow the Left to grasp the Islamization project as class struggle. In other words, they failed to interpret the attack on women as a full assault on the working class, both women and men. The Left's analysis of the regime's rhetoric of anti-US imperialism also revealed their economistic/workerist approach in which the dialectics of the inner-relations of religion, patriarchy, and capitalism was obscured in the simplistic binary of the internal/external enemy. Still, although 'the woman question' was given a secondary status, thousands of women persisted in their resistance and fought the theocratic regime without a clear political agenda, and thousands were imprisoned in the 1980s and thousands were forced into exile.

Coming to the end of an endless story about the struggle for women's emancipation, I have arrived at the conclusion that the capitalist and patriarchal order today is an obstacle not only to women's emancipation, but together with it, to human emancipation. I see neither in today's Marxist theory nor in feminist theory much hope for making history through what Ovington called the abolition of poverty and the destruction of servitude among women. There is increasing interest in Marxism in the wake of the continuing economic crisis of capitalism; however, Marxism needs an overhaul, a serious renewal which involves, in part, a dialectical understanding of what Engels called the first great divide in history – the division of human society into two genders that form a hierarchical, patriarchal system.

OVERCOMING THE HYPHENATION IN MARXIST-FEMINISM

The life story briefly and partially charted above implies that a century of struggle for linking the two major emancipatory projects, Marxism and feminism, involved more than a preoccupation with theoretical interests. It provides evidence about the way in which resistance against patriarchy in a country like Iran is inseparable from the rest of the world. This struggle is rooted in the material and intellectual conditions that have emerged since the nineteenth century as well as world-wide resistance to class and gender rule. This story reveals both the universality and particularity of oppression (gender, race, ethnicity, etc.), its political and ideological character, as well as the internationalization of feminist knowledge and women's struggle for emancipation. This account calls into question nativist, nationalist, and religious reductions of social relations of gender to questions of identity. Theory and politics are products of an international division of labour in which capitalism – patriarchy – racism rules.

I have pointed so far to two conflictual trends – one that is theoretical and moves away from synthesizing feminism and Marxism, the other political, that is, the escalating gender oppression and class exploitation that calls out for a blending of the two. In hyphenated relations since the 1960s, Marxism and feminism have coexisted, debated, interacted, and maintained their realms. In fact, with or without hyphenation, the two worldviews have shaped each other since the end of the nineteenth century without creating a theoretical breakthrough. A glimpse of this history reveals flexibility for renovation and inclusion more in Marxism than in feminism. Marxism since its inception has incorporated many advances in the (social) sciences, for example, Marx and Engels' integration of Darwin's theory of evolution or Henry Lewis Morgan's anthropological work, or Lenin's embracing of John Hobson's study of imperialism, which amounted to a major shift in Marxist theory of capitalism and the strategy for socialist revolution. In fact, this kind of liaison between Marxism and non-Marxist knowledge and art was underscored by Mao when he emphasized that Marxism 'embraces but cannot replace', for instance, realism in art or theory in physics.[14]

One may argue along the same lines that Marxism should embrace feminist contributions to the understanding of patriarchy. Feminisms come with their own dynamics, social bases, theories, methodologies, ideologies, epistemologies, and visions. Marxism's emphasis on oppression and exploitation appeals to some feminists while the epistemological and methodological persuasions of many feminists are in conflict with dialectics, which distinguishes Marxism from other social theories. Feminist theories are, thus, in a difficult position for absorbing Marxism. In addition to theoretical and epistemological incongruity, the political repression of Marxism has left its mark on the theoretical front. For instance, in the wake of the restoration of capitalism in China and the fall of the Soviet Union, many socialist-feminists or feminist Marxists abandoned Marxism,[15] and those still committed to the critique of capitalism tend to identify

[14] Mao Tsetung, 'Talks at the Yenan Forum on Literature and Art', *Selected Readings from the Works of Mao Tsetung*, Peking: Foreign Languages Press, 1971, p. 281.

[15] For instance, Claudie Broyelle, who wrote enthusiastically about progress in dismantling patriarchal gender relations in the wake of the Cultural Revolution in China, failed to make sense of the restoration of capitalism and retracted her writings. C. Broyelle, *Women's Liberation in China*, Atlantic Highlands: Humanities Press, 1977 and then, C. Broyelle, J. Broyelle and E. Tschirhart, *China: A Second Look*, Atlantic Highlands: Humanities Press, 1980.

themselves as 'materialist feminists'. Materialism, in this context, is often taken to mean 'political economy', which is placed in opposition to 'culture', 'language', or 'discourse'. However, this understanding of matter and materialism is not Marxist in so far as Marxism understands matter as 'the external reality', that is, all that exists outside our mind, thus forming a dialectical relationship of unity and struggle with consciousness; in this philosophical understanding, all cultural, linguistic, and 'spiritual' phenomena are, like economic relations, also part of matter or of material or external reality.

My inclination to remove the hyphen in Marxist-feminism should not be interpreted as a desire for parting the two. Rather, I have tried to delineate a more constructive and enduring relationship between these two major realms of knowledge, two sites of struggle, and two horizons of emancipation. Inessa Armand (1874–1920), the Russian Marxist feminist, said what many Marxists have repeatedly said in different words and contexts: 'If the emancipation of women is unthinkable without communism, then communism is unthinkable without the full emancipation of women'.[16] There was no illusion, at least in theory, about the intricate nature of emancipation.

Armand and Ovington realized, theoretically, that 'servitude' and 'poverty' would not end within the framework of the regime of bourgeois rights. Equally significant is Lenin's repeated emphasis, after the 1917 revolution, that the full legal equality of women and men immediately granted by the Soviet government could not and would not bring about extra-legal (social and economic) equality overnight, a goal which could be achieved only 'in the complete triumph of

[16] B. Clements, *Bolshevik Feminist: The Life of Alexandra Kollantai*, Bloomington: Indian University Press, 1979, p. 155.

communism' (Lenin 1982: 84-85). This view is rooted in a historical materialist understanding of the past and future and of the nature of socialist revolution, which treats the equality of genders, classes, races, or nations not as a legal question but more profoundly as also social and economic. Building on Marx, Lenin emphasized that socialism is a long period of transition between capitalism and communism, and necessarily combines the features and properties of both systems. Socialism is, in this understanding, a class society, in which the proletariat is the ruling class holding a vision to eventually abolish itself – and all classes – through protracted class struggle (Lenin 1971: 295). The restoration of capitalism in the USSR in 1956 led Mao to theorize the dynamics of class struggle in socialism; he emphasized that the communist party, itself a product of class society and the site where a 'new bourgeoisie', is the main ideological and political source for the restoration of capitalism. In these theorizations, (re-) production in capitalism is exceedingly complex, and this mode of production does not readily lend itself to transformation into communism. In sharp contrast to this view, we find more recent theorizations of communism as a new order that is already emerging more or less spontaneously without recourse to revolution and, commanded by the dynamics of capitalism transformed into 'Empire', through new production and labour processes.[17] All of this points to momentous theoretical and political struggles under conditions of unceasing change in the contemporary capitalist world order. Today, interpreting the past and present and charting the future is a heavy burden on both Marxists and feminists.

I opened this essay by reminding us of the imperialist war of a century ago, when a new phase in the colonization and re-

[17] These are the ideas of M. Hardt and T. Negri in *Empire* (2000) and *Multitude* (2004).

division of Africa, Asia, and Latin America began. Consider the massacre of Gaza by the settler colonial and Zionist state of Israel which only came into existence in 1948 through the forced expulsion and dispossession of the Palestinian population. The birth of the state of Israel is known to Palestinians as *Nakba Day* (the Day of the Catastrophe). Thinking through the horror of our time, a world that is messy, chaotic, and riddled with injustice, violence, war, and lawlessness, I observe traces of an order in this anarchy. At the core of this (dis-) order is the logic of patriarchal racist capitalism/imperialism, in which women's bodies and sexuality are its battleground. In this anarchical social (dis-) order, women inhabit contradictory relations of being the subject/object, possessors/dispossessors, or saviours/betrayers of culture and social relations; this social disorder creates both the condition of women's liberation and of their subjugation.

Resistance to this colonial order and to the states carved up by imperialist powers out of the remnants of older empires began immediately and everywhere on the three continents – and continues in our time. Women participated, actively and on a mass scale, in the uprisings in Arab countries that began in December 2010 in Tunisia and spread throughout Middle East and North Africa. They were organizers, leaders, and cyber-activists. However, most women did not take part in these protests as members of organized women's movements demanding the dismantling of patriarchal gender relations. They, together with males and side by side with them, called for the replacement of dictators with parliamentary democracy and thus left the socio-economic system and the class structure intact. Even worse was the centre-less and leaderless politics that was proudly advocated by many, including secular youth groups. While the poverty-stricken majority did not gain any ground, women lost even more as they were subjected to male violence even in the streets and squares. Within a period of two years, the dictators were toppled in Tunisia, Egypt, Yemen, and Libya and were succeeded by well-organized groups advocating another form of dictatorship in the form of theocracy. Not long after in Egypt – the main centre of political power in the Middle East and North Africa – the army ignored the popular quest for parliamentarianism and installed a military dictator at the helm of the state. In Syria, the diverse groups opposed to Assad's regime relied on regional and imperialist powers for military and political support. Within a year, the country turned into a battlefield between the Assad regime, Islamic fundamentalists, Western imperialism, and Arab and Islamic states in the region. In the absence of revolutionary politics, the uprisings led to yet more theocratic rule in which women, the labouring masses, ethnic and religious minorities, and freedom of opinion and association were seriously threatened. It seemed as if people in the Arab streets were replicating the 1979 Iranian revolution. In the case of both the Iranian Revolution and the so-called 'Arab Spring,' the absence of revolutionary consciousness – that is, theory, politics, and organizing – made it possible for imperialism and Islamic fundamentalism to suppress any struggle for revolutionary change. The conflict and co-existence of these two obsolete forces have devastated the peoples and countries of the Middle East and North Africa. Here as elsewhere in the world, women and men are ready for a transformation of this horrible reality into a bright future for the majority of the people. However, consciousness or subjective factors lag behind objective reality, playing into the hands of a minority who have monopolized violence as well as political and economic power.

CONTRIBUTORS

Amar Farooqui is Professor of History at the University of Delhi.

B. T. Ranadive (1904-1990) was a leader of the Communist Party of India (Marxist) and the General Secretary of the Centre for Indian Trade Unions.

Irfan Habib is Professor Emeritus at the Department of History at Aligarh Muslim University and the author of many essential books on Indian history and Marxism, including his monumental *People's History of India* series.

Jodi Dean is a Professor of Political Science at Hobart & William Smith College. She is the author of *The Communist Horizon* (2012) and *Crowds and Party* (2016).

Prabhat Patnaik held the Sukhamoy Charvarty Chair at the Centre for Economic Studies and Planning at the Jawaharlal Nehru University and was vice chairman of the Planning Board of Kerala. He is the author of a number of important books on Marxist theory and is the editor of *Social Scientist.*

Prabir Purkayastha is the editor of Newsclick.

Prakash Karat is a former General Secretary of the Communist Party of India (Marxist).

Shahrzad Mojab is a Professor at the University of Toronto. Her essay draws from her introduction to *Marxism and Feminism*, a 2015 book that she edited.

Sitaram Yechury is the General Secretary of the Communist Party of India (Marxist) and a member of the Rajya Sabha.

Vijay Prashad is the Chief Editor of LeftWord Books.

ACKNOWLEDGEMENTS

Vijay Prashad, Introduction, original for this volume.

Irfan Habib, The Road to the October Revolution in Russia, 1917, *The Marxist*, Vol. XXXII, no. 4, October-December 2016.

Amar Farooqui, The October Revolution and the National Movement in India, *The Marxist*, Vol. XXXII, no. 4, October-December 2016.

B. T. Ranadive, Seventy Glorious Years: Achievements & Problems, *The Marxist*, Vol. V, October-December 1987.

Prakash Karat, The Gorbachevian Reforms: Dismantling the Communist Party, *The Marxist*, Vol. IX, nos. 3-4, July-December 1991.

Sitaram Yechury, Economy: Reforms for Restoration of Capitalism, *The Marxist*, Vol. IX, nos. 3-4, July-December 1991.

Prabhat Patnaik, Globalization and the Impasse of Capitalism, Harold Wolpe memorial lecture, University of Witswatersrand, Johannesburg, 27 October 2016.

Jodi Dean, The Party and the Communist Horizon, original for this volume.

Prabir Purkayastha, Remembering the October Revolution by Rebuilding the Socialist Imagination, original for this volume.

Shahrzad Mojab, Marxism, Feminism & Revolution, revized version of the introduction to *Marxism and Feminism*, ed. Shahrzad Mojab, Zed Books, 2015.